Gently with the Innocents

Alan Hunter

ROBINSON

Constable & Robinson Ltd
55–56 Russell Square
London WC1B 4HP
www.constablerobinson.com

First published in the UK by Cassell & Company Ltd., 1970

This paperback edition published by Robinson,
an imprint of Constable & Robinson Ltd., 2013

A copy of the British Library Cataloguing in Publication
Data is available from the British Library

ISBN 978-1-78033-945-0 (paperback)
ISBN 978-1-47210-463-2 (ebook)

Typeset by TW Typesetting, Plymouth, Devon

Printed and bound by CPI Group (UK) Ltd, Croydon, CR0 4YY

3 5 7 9 10 8 6 4 2

Let me add to the above legend that 'Harrisons' is a real
house. For the purpose of the narrative I removed it
from its village and placed it in the town I have called
Cross, but a little detective work with this book and a
map may suggest its location to the curious. The
quotation given in the text is only slightly doctored,
and the description of the house is accurate – except
for one minor feature.

The house was for sale when I explored it. I believe
the price asked was very reasonable.

A. H.

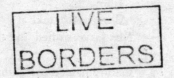

CHAPTER ONE

T HE TELEPHONE RANG out in the hall and Gently looked up frowning. Praise the Lord, not tonight – after the sort of day he'd been having!

In Elphinstone Road the rain was still pelting as it had been pelting all day: that chill, penetrating stuff which they kept for the back-end of November. He'd come in sodden, feeling old, and had downed a couple of rum-and-lemons. Mrs Jarvis was out. He'd had to knock himself up a poached egg and a pot of tea.

Now, settled by the fire in his den, he was beginning to feel dry at last, and he didn't want to know about Assistant Commissioners with bad cases of murder on their minds.

'For you, sir.'

Mrs Jarvis poked her unexpressive face round the door.

'Who is it?'

'Didn't catch his name, sir. Ain't none of your lot by the sound of him.'

She'd just come in. Her head was swathed in a glinting pixie-hood of grey plastic.

'All right, I'll take it.'

Mrs Jarvis sniffed and drew her head back from the door.

Gently hauled the extension phone over.

'Chief Superintendent Gently . . .'

For a moment he could hear nothing but the sound of irregular breathing.

'Yes?'

'I . . . I . . .'

'Speak up!'

'I—please, I want to talk to you.'

'Who are you?'

The name sounded like 'piecemeal': no wonder Mrs Jarvis didn't get it.

'So what's the trouble?'

'It's . . . the police . . .'

'Yes?'

'They think I've murdered my uncle.'

Gently sighed. 'And did you?' he asked.

'No!'

'So why bother me?'

There were confused sounds at the other end, as though the caller were shifting his grip on the receiver. Gently could hear traffic. The man was probably in a call-box.

'Look, I must talk to you . . . please! It isn't as simple as it sounds. Fazakerly told me—'

'Fazakerly?'

'Yes. He said you were related . . .'

Gently grimaced. John Fazakerly was a remote connection of his sister's husband – a ne'er-do-well who had dragged Gently into a case that was none of his business. Not much of a recommendation to quote.

'I don't know him, of course . . . my firm sold the lease of his flat. But he'd mentioned you . . . about his wife . . . and I had to talk to someone . . .'

'And he suggested me.'

'Yes.'

'Surely a lawyer would be more appropriate?'

'But you don't understand!'

Gently yawned.

'He said . . . if I were innocent . . . come to you.'

A chunk of coal fell against the bars and lay hissing a geyser of white smoke. In the phone Gently distinctly heard gears being changed. Traffic lights? A junction?

'Where are you speaking from?'

'I'm in a call-box. At Tally-Ho Corner.'

'I see.'

'Please! If you could give me just ten minutes . . .'

Gently shrugged at nobody. 'Well, since you're out here.'

'I can see you?'

'For what it's worth.'

'Thanks . . . oh, thanks!'

Gently dropped the phone with a grunt.

His name was Peachment, Adrian Peachment, and he gave his age as twenty-six, a rather fey-looking young man with dark hair and shining dark eyes. Not a Londoner. Even over the phone you could spot a broadness in his speech. Yet he dressed in the current semi-military vogue and wore his hair in a nest that

3

brushed his collar. He had parked a Mini with a recent date-letter under the tear-drop lamp across the street.

'I'm terribly grateful, sir . . .'

He had left with Mrs Jarvis a short alpaca coat and a deer-stalker.

'Oh, sit down.'

'I wouldn't have imposed—'

'Do you smoke?'

He lit a cigarette jerkily, using a butane lighter.

Gently himself lit his pipe.

'First, your troubles are none of my business. If the police are dealing with your case I couldn't interfere anyway.'

'It isn't that—'

'Listen to me! You'll probably only make matters worse. If you drop something I shall have to report it. You'd be far better off if you talked to your lawyer. You have one, haven't you?'

'Well . . . no.'

'Why not?'

'At this stage . . . I didn't think . . .'

'What do you mean – "at this stage"?'

'The coroner . . . at the inquest they seemed satisfied.'

Gently breathed smoke, staring at him.

'Didn't you say you were under suspicion?'

'Yes.' Peachment flicked his cigarette nervously. 'Only the coroner . . . they're not sure it was murder.'

Not sure it was murder! Gently chewed on his pipe-stem, eyeing the young man with little friendliness. For this he'd interrupted his snug evening, and the book lying open on the side-table . . .

'Just give me the facts.'

'Yes, of course.'

Peachment sat like a woman, his knitted legs turned sideways. He had a young-old face, long, hollow-cheeked, and long-fingered hands with bony joints.

'You see, they found him dead . . . actually, the milkman . . .'

'Who?'

'My uncle, James Peachment. He was seventy, you know, and living alone. They found him dead at the foot of some stairs.'

'In London?'

'No. No, in Cross . . . that's a little town on the Northshire border. Uncle always lived there . . . my family . . . I'm up here now, I've a job in Kensington.'

'What did the report say?'

'A fractured skull.'

'So?'

Peachment jigged his cigarette. 'There was other bruising. On the arms, legs, everywhere. As though someone had beaten the old boy up.'

Gently puffed slowly. 'This happened in his house?'

'Yes. It's a queer old place called Harrisons. Elizabethan, something like that. All beams and passages and funny rooms. Well, the milkman found him at the foot of this staircase. It only goes to an empty room. And nothing taken as far as I knew . . . they made me go through the place, to check.'

'Had it been broken into?'

Peachment shook his head. 'They wouldn't need to

break in if they knew the place. One of the back doors opens into a lean-to and doesn't even have a bolt. Of course it's mad . . . but that's in the country. People don't bother so much there.'

'Carry on.'

'Well . . . the police were awkward. You see, I was down there the day it happened. My girl-friend lives there. I called on Uncle. They got my finger-prints off one of the door-knobs. Then there's the bit about me inheriting – my people are dead, so it comes to me. And, well . . . I don't have a very good alibi, either. You can see their point. I could have done it.'

Gently eased himself back in his favourite chair. Perhaps there was something in it, after all! With a case like that lined-up against him, you might excuse any man for getting jumpy.

'What is your alibi, just for the record?'

Peachment's neck was flushing a little.

'Actually . . . Jeanie and I had a row. I cleared off back here not long after tea.'

'And that doesn't cover you?'

'No, not really. They say he died about eight p.m. Well, I wasn't back here till close on ten, and nobody saw me get in anyway. You see, I have a flat.'

Yes, indeed, Gently saw. He blew a couple of casual smoke-rings and gazed at Peachment almost benignly.

'But they haven't arrested you?'

'Well . . . no. I mean, the coroner returned an open verdict. Uncle could have got the bruises falling down the stairs – he *could* have done. It's just possible.'

'Then what's your worry?'

Peachment's eyes widened. 'The police don't think he died by accident.'

'What about you?'

'I *know* he didn't. And that's why I wanted to talk to you.'

He felt carefully in his breast pocket and took out a small, folded manila envelope.

'This is why Uncle was murdered,' he said. 'And the reason why they beat him up.'

Gently took the envelope. The long fingers were trembling as they handed it over. Though small, and folded smaller, the envelope was unexpectedly heavy. Gently weighed it in his hand a moment.

'A coin?'

'A medal actually . . . that one.'

'You mean there are others?'

'Yes. I'm sure of it. But that's the only one left.'

Peachment leant forward, watching closely while Gently slid the contents from the envelope. It contained a rather crude gold medallion, not quite geometrically round. On the face was the bust of a large-nosed man surrounded by a semi-legible inscription in Latin, on the verso a dove and a wreath of laurel leaves. It was about as large as a crown.

'Careful . . . please!' Peachment whispered.

Gently shrugged. 'What's it worth?'

'Something over a thousand . . . I've just had it valued. It's a Papal medal of Innocent III.'

'Nice,' Gently said. 'And there were more?'

'Yes, more. A lot more. I found that one hidden in

7

the book-room at Harrisons – whoever killed him didn't find it.'

Gently laid the medal on the side-table. Really, this case had got some life in it! People had been killed, and would be again, for much less than the price of that single gold piece. He looked at Peachment. Peachment was anxiously gazing at the medal lying on the table.

'It's Extremely Fine, you see. If you scratched it—'

'What makes you think there are more?'

'The legend, of course.'

'The legend!'

'Yes.' Peachment's eyes jerked to his almost indignantly. 'There's a legend about Harrisons – I told you, it's a queer sort of old place. There's supposed to be treasure hidden in it. A hoard of gold. Anyone'll tell you.'

'And that – that's part of it?'

Peachment nodded. 'How else could Uncle have got that medal? He could never have bought it – they're rare anyway – and Uncle didn't have that sort of money.'

'Let's get this straight,' Gently said. He took a few short puffs. 'Are there any grounds for this beautiful fable, or is it just the usual village tale?'

'I believe it—'

'Very likely! But is it backed by any facts?'

Peachment shrugged his lean shoulders feebly. 'Actually . . . if you put it like that . . .'

'Just so.'

'But wait a minute. There's something else I have to tell you. It's the way Uncle behaved that last afternoon. He was . . . you know . . . excited about something.'

'Go on.'

'Yes,' Peachment said. 'Excited. At the time I didn't really notice. It was just a duty visit. I was impatient – wanted to get back to Jeanie. He was' – Peachment's large hand sawed – 'all . . . bubbling, you understand? Like – like a cat who's swallowed a canary. He kept smiling and grinning to himself.

'Then there's what he said as I was leaving . . . oh, I know it's nothing to go on! But it was the way he held on to my hand, the sort of triumphant look he gave me.'

'And what did he say?'

'He said, "Boy, don't sell this place when I'm gone. There's more here than dust and old rotten beams." And he kept shaking my hand all the time.'

'Hm.'

Gently took more puffs. Did Peachment honestly think he would swallow this? Perhaps the young man was realizing how thin it sounded, because he added earnestly, 'I'm sure . . . positive . . .'

Gently grunted.

'So this is the theory. Your uncle had found a hoard of gold. He keeps it to himself, but someone finds out, and they beat him up to make him tell where he's hidden it.'

'Yes – that's it.'

'And this is all your evidence?'

'The medal – yes. But where else . . . ?'

'It's too thin.'

'But the medal . . . I tell you—'

'You should have shown the medal to the local police.'

Peachment's dark eyes rounded despairingly.

'Look, sir, I know – I *know* I'm right! That medal's a rarity. I took it to Seaby's. They say there's only two more like it. I didn't take it to the local police because . . . well, they're against me enough now. But Uncle was murdered, and there has to be a reason – and that's the reason. I *know.*'

Gently picked up the medal again. Its rough heaviness was convincing. Purely as gold . . . Perhaps the medal, anyway, deserved a little looking into.

'Who was your uncle?'

'He – he was nobody.'

Again the anxious look as Gently fondled the medal.

'What was his job?'

'He kept the harness-shop. But he retired from that ten years ago.'

'He owned – what was it – Harrisons?'

'Yes. He and Aunt Agatha had always lived there. She died soon after he retired. He lived all alone. A bit . . . eccentric.'

'He didn't collect these things?'

'Good Lord, no! He's got a few old books and things.'

'What sort of books?'

'Nothing on coins. Old books on horses, local history.'

'Are you in possession?'

'Well . . . more or less. He didn't leave any will. There's still some lawyer's business to go through. All this happened a month ago.'

'Did he have many friends?'

'No . . . I told you. He lived alone, scarcely saw anyone.'

'Housekeeper? Char?'

Peachment shook his head. 'A recluse . . . that's the word I wanted.'

'So you've no idea who might have killed him?'

Peachment said bitterly, 'I'm the suspect.'

'Right.' Gently put down the medal. He drew out his pocket-book and began scribbling. 'Here's your receipt. I'll keep the medal. I'll see that proper inquiries are made.'

'You're going to . . . keep it?' Peachment looked dismayed.

'Of course. Like you, I'm curious about its provenance.'

'But—'

'Well?'

'It's all right, I suppose . . . only, please . . .'

'I'll take care it's properly handled.'

He took a note of Peachment's address. The young man lived at St John's Gate. He worked for Lutyen and Marshall, estate agents, a large firm of good standing.

At the door he hesitated, then stuck out his hand. 'I'm grateful, really . . . I mean, suspected like that.'

'Don't be so sure you're out of the wood.'

'Fazakerly was right . . .'

Gently said nothing.

He came back into the den and stood some moments by the fire. Outside he could hear the Mini being started and, after some buzzing, being driven away. A curious business, an odd young man! An old man's face on young shoulders. One could see through it to the recluse uncle, the lonely old harness-maker in his mouldering house. A medieval face . . . and a medieval coin – or did Innocent III go back yet further?

Gently relit his pipe. But was there in fact a case here? Old men did fall down stairs and die. A fractured skull, a clutch of bruises, they were sufficiently commonplace in such an event. The locals, anyway, hadn't pushed the matter, as they would if there had been evidence of theft. And the coroner, obviously he'd been satisfied . . . only uncertain about how the old man came to fall.

Just one of those tragedies that happen too often to the elderly who live alone.

And yet . . . he stared again at the thick, bulge-edged medal, with its grotesque portrait, its uneven lettering.

Coming to a decision, he hooked up the phone.

'Trunks. I want Merely 25. It's a Northshire number.'

As he stood waiting he could hear the rain beating faster and a drop or two hissed on the coals in the grate.

'Merely 25.'

'Superintendent Gently.'

'Good Heavens . . . Gently!'

He took the phone to his chair. Sir Daynes Broke, the Northshire Chief Constable, rarely came to business in the first five minutes.

'. . . my first twenty-pounder on Sunday . . . live-bait, y'know, no twiddling with spoons . . . Gwen's

12

here, she'll want a word with you . . . when are you coming for a day with the pike? . . .'

Then at last, as an afterthought: 'You're ringing about something . . . ?'

Gently gave him a summary of what Peachment had told him. Sir Daynes listened with little cluckings, but didn't interrupt till Gently had finished.

'Yes, well . . . know about it, of course. Fact, Lindsay, the coroner, is a chum of mine. Says there's no doubt the old fellow took a tumble – thin skull, y'know. He was getting on.'

'And the local Superintendent?'

'Chief Inspector. Fellow called Boyland. He's all right. He's not too happy, but there's nothing to go on. Doesn't like the nephew – that's a fact.'

'What about this treasure?'

'Oh, poppycock. Stories like that about Merely Manor.'

'But there is this medal.'

'Won't be worth much. I collect them, y'know. What d'you say it is?'

Gently told him. There was a slight pause at the Merely end of the phone.

'Innocent III?'

'So Peachment says. And the inscription reads INNOCENTI III.'

'Describe it to me.'

Gently described it. He had a feeling that Sir Daynes was holding his breath.

'That's dashed queer.'

'Is it worth much?'

'My dear Gently, it's almost priceless. There are only two or three known examples. How did old Peachment get his hands on one?'

Gently smiled at the spitting fire. This was young Peachment over again! But clearly the old harness-maker's house at Cross held one mystery. Unless . . .

'Of course, we've only the nephew's word about where he got it.'

The phone made irritable noises.

'Doesn't matter where he got it, man. We still want to know where it came from.'

'It's in Extremely Fine condition.'

'You're making my blasted mouth water!'

'But doesn't that suggest . . . say, a collection?'

'Now you're making a little sense.'

Gently prodded the medal where it lay on its envelope.

'I'll check, of course, if one is missing. Seaby's will know where they are . . . if there are only three, it shouldn't take long. But suppose none of the known ones are missing?'

'Then you'll grill that nephew silly.'

'But if he's telling the truth?'

Sir Daynes made throat-noises. 'Yes . . . begin to see what you mean.'

'A collection . . . a fabulous collection . . . perhaps other semi-unique pieces. Maybe nothing to do with the legend, but certainly something to do with Peachment.'

'But a theft like that—'

'It may not yet have been discovered.'

'But there'd be records of such a collection.'

'Not if it were put together illicitly by someone buying stolen coins.'

Sir Daynes honked and hawed a little. The smile was still on Gently's face.

'So what do we do, man?'

'It's up to you. I think, on balance, perhaps Peachment was murdered.'

'Hrmph! And I'd certainly like to see that medal.'

'I could bring it along. If I got the case.'

When he hung up the smile was a grin. He poured himself a Cognac and sat down to drink it. Then he picked up the phone again, raked off a number, propped the receiver under his chin.

'Gently . . . send me a car, will you? I have some property that should be under lock and key.'

Half an hour later, when the car arrived, the rain was changing into snow.

CHAPTER TWO

CROSS WAS A slushy, two-and-a-half-hour drive up the A's 12 and 140, with dimmed headlights and wipers grinding at a dirty mist all the way. You turned off at Broome, a village with a handsome coaching-inn, and a murderous mile later ran into the outskirts of the little town.

On another day it would have been charming. It was built on a slope beside a small lake. Across the lake you saw Georgian houses forming a crescent around the lake shore.

Water Street, the principal thoroughfare, spread out and divided at the top of the slope, showing off handsome gables and facades and the Ionic portico of the Corn Exchange.

A piece of Old England! But you needed to come back in June. Just now it was huddled in a dirty gloom which the glowing shop windows seemed to make more dreary. Pedestrians' breath smoked and they pulled away from cars that hissed past the narrow pavements. A few grimy pigeons huddled into the nooks of the Corn Exchange.

Gently held second all the way up Water Street, where vans parked regardless of yellow lines. At the top he pulled in beside a fishmonger's. The man at the slab was grinning with cold.

'Where's the police station?'

'Keep a-goin'. Take the second on the left.'

He stared curiously for a moment, then turned and began jigging and chafing his fingers.

The police station was a worn-out building with a date on a plaque, 1905. It was built of dark red brick and an inferior freestone which was flaking off round doors and windows. Gently parked in a slot near the steps. He entered a dank hall with a tiled floor. A huge, bulging, green-painted radiator stood clear of the wall and wheezed unhappily.

'I'd like to speak to Chief Inspector Boyland.'

The young constable at the desk was slow to attend to him. Then, learning his name, he blushed childishly and collided with a chair as he came round the desk.

'This way, sir. I'll just . . .'

They went down a corridor laid with balding blue lino. The constable tapped hastily at the door at the end, opened it a little to hiss, 'Sir . . . he's arrived, sir!'

Gently went in.

'Inspector Gissing. He's in charge of the case.'

Gently shook hands with a heavy-faced, benevolent-looking man. Boyland himself was plump and jowled and had a thin moustache which looked out of place.

'This business about a medal . . .'

They'd both been drinking beer, though the glasses

17

had been hurriedly pushed to one side. A plate with crumbs on it lay on the desk. Presumably Gently had disturbed their elevenses.

'It's a bit out of character, don't you think? I mean, old Peachment wasn't worth a bean. There's only the house, and that's falling down.'

He was plainly embarrassed and trying to talk his way out of it.

'Any more of that beer?'

'What . . . what . . . ?'

'I'm feeling a bit dry after my drive.'

Boyland stared at him round-eyed a moment, then chuckled and pulled open a drawer of his desk.

'Sorry . . . didn't know . . . you being such a nob.'

'And a couple of sandwiches would go down.'

In the end he was sitting in Boyland's chair with a glass of nut-brown and a full plate beside him, while Boyland sprawled fatly on the edge of the desk and Gissing leant comfortably against a radiator.

'Let me put you in the picture. I've had another long chat with young Peachment. I can't shake his story about finding the medal. I think we'll just have to accept it.'

'Well, I don't know,' Boyland said dubiously.

'Naturally, I've done some checking on Peachment. He seems to be a fairly clean-living young man. No trouble with us. No doubtful acquaintances.'

'Have you checked on his alibi, sir?' Gissing asked.

'Yes. He was back in his flat by ten p.m.'

Gissing's eyes were blank. 'He could have done it,' he said. 'It's running it close . . . but he could have.'

Gently drank a mouthful of nut-brown.

'Just for the moment, let's leave him in the clear. He's telling a straight story about his movements, about finding the medal in his uncle's book-room. Now, if the theory's right, someone knew about that medal, and that's why Peachment was beaten up. What I want is a list of people who were friends or associates of the dead man.'

Boyland shook his head. 'Won't be easy. Peachment didn't have any chums.'

'People he talked to.'

'That's just it. He never gave time of day to anyone.'

'He was a rum 'un, sir,' Gissing put in. 'After his wife died he sort of closed up. You'd see him ambling around and muttering to himself; but he'd never speak a word to you.'

'What about tradesmen?'

'There's the milkman,' Gissing said. 'It was him who went in and found the body. But he was in bed asleep when Peachment was killed – I checked him out. His family vouch for him.'

'Other tradesmen?'

'Nobody delivered. He'd buy his bits and pieces out.'

'Doctor?'

'He was on Doctor Paley's list, but I don't think the Doctor ever visited him.'

'And he didn't have any neighbours,' Boyland said. 'He was the only resident in Frenze Street. It's the livestock market down there, and Hampton's warehouse, and some other old properties.'

Gently drank some more nut-brown. Almost, you felt, they were trying to be unhelpful! If there was a murderer going loose, they didn't want him pinned to the comfortable, crime-free town of Cross. Whereas young Peachment . . .

'Where's the PM report?'

Boyland slid off the desk and fetched it for him. It listed twenty-seven separate bruises on different parts of Peachment's body. They were indifferently distributed about arms, legs, body, face, and only two were described as severe. The fractured skull presumably came from the stairs.

'Anything strike you about this?'

Boyland's stare was non-committal.

'I saw the corpse, sir,' Gissing said. 'There were too many bruises there for a tumble.'

'But the bruises themselves?'

'Well . . . all over him, sir. Only light bruises, most of them.'

'If a man were being beaten to extract information would you expect bruising like that?'

Gissing's eyes went blank. Then he slowly shook his head.

'You'd expect them more . . . localized, sir,' he said.

'And more severe?'

'Yes, sir. More severe. I don't think he was duffed up to make him talk.'

'Then why was he beaten?'

Gissing's head kept shaking. 'It struck me as queer at the time, sir. Maybe revenge . . . something like that. All I know is they weren't an accident.'

'Maybe a nutter,' Boyland said.

'You have any nutters?' Gently asked.

Boyland shrugged his plump shoulders. Clearly he wasn't going to admit that!

About the legend of the gold hoard they were derisive. It was going around when Boyland was a kid. Wasn't there always a tale of that sort about old houses like Harrisons? A queer old house, a queer old man – to the kids, he'd never be less than a miser. Gissing, who'd poked about the place pretty thoroughly, discounted the notion of a secret hiding-place.

'You went through the book-room when you were there?'

'Yes, sir. At least, there's a room with books in it.'

'Young Peachment says the medal was in a drawer in the book-room.'

'Well, sir . . . actually, I was looking for a blunt instrument.'

'What about the drawer?'

There were a couple of drawers. Gissing had glanced in and seen old papers. He had rustled them with his hand, found nothing sinister, closed the drawers and passed on.

'So the medal might have been there?'

Yes, it might have been, folded away in its manila envelope. Which envelope Gently had sent down to the lab and had received a report on that left him no wiser.

He told them about the medal. He'd taken it back to Seaby's, who of course remembered young Peachment bringing it in. As soon as Peachment had gone they'd done their own checking – none of the known Innocent III medals was missing. Two were in museums, in London and New York; the third belonged to a Greek millionaire. Gently had nailed them down to a valuation of fourteen hundred, though in an auction it might go higher.

'And this is it.'

He laid the medal on the desk. They gazed at its heavy disc in silence.

That was what had been under the old bills, and what Gissing had nearly put his hand on . . .

'Any coin-collectors in the town?'

He knew that would be a forlorn hope.

'There's Bressingham . . . he keeps an antique shop. But he wouldn't stock anything like this.'

'I'll talk to him. He might know something.'

'This knocks me all of a heap,' Boyland said. 'If old Peachment had one of these, why not a dozen, or a score?'

'The hoard of gold, sir,' Gissing said.

'Meanwhile,' Gently said, 'this one. If there's nothing else you can think of to tell me, I'd like to go along and look at the house.'

They watched with the same, childlike silence as he wrapped up the medal again in its tissue.

'If there's room in your safe . . .'

'Of course.'

Boyland hastened to unlock the old, double-doored Chubb, which stood in a corner.

'You'd like a receipt?'

'I'll trust you this time.'

22

Boyland took the medal into his two hands, handling it as though he thought it might burn him.

A clock struck somewhere in the gloom as Gently and Gissing came out of the police station. It was noon, but it might have been any hour of what passed for daylight at the end of November.

They snuggled gratefully into Gently's Sceptre, still a little warm from the drive down. Gissing had donned a hefty tweed greatcoat of a style that Gently hadn't seen for years.

'Have you had any snow here?'

'Two nights ago. We'll be getting some more soon.'

'What sort of weather was it when Peachment was killed?'

Gissing thought a moment, then said, 'A mild spell.'

He directed Gently back down Water Street and then left past a car park. A further left turn brought them into a narrow street with a sale-ground and cattle-pens along one side. Opposite was a terrace of old straw-thatched cottages, their thatch moulting, windows boarded; beyond, and set back, steep pantiled gables, and finally a dreary red-brick depository warehouse.

'Frenze Street . . . it's pretty old.'

Gently grunted, let the Sceptre coast.

'Before they built the market there were a lot of old houses . . . looked like something out of Dickens.'

'A cul-de-sac?'

'Yes. There's a footway through to Thingoe Road.'

'Cars park here at night?'

'Never seen many. The park we went past is free.'

Even now Frenze Street had atmosphere, with the best part of its glories gone. It was slightly dog-legged, a little sloped. Its buildings seemed watchful in the misty twilight. Pretty old . . . A spirit of age had taken root in the place.

'Here's Harrisons.'

It was the house of the pantiled gables, at the very end of the street and butting on to the warehouse yard. A [-shaped Elizabethan house, with the two gable-fronts of unequal size. The wings were apparently of three storeys and the central portion of two. There were a number of irregular small windows. The front had been rendered with a drab plaster. It stood withdrawn from the street behind rusting palings and a tangle of dead willow-herb, nettles and rank grass.

'Goes back a bit, wouldn't you say?'

Above the steep roofs were tall, twisted brick chimneys. One of them had been rebuilt at some stage. The other was an original Tudor chimney.

'Why is it called Harrisons?'

Gissing shrugged. 'Name of the bloke who built it, I reckon.'

'It's not on record?'

'Not to my knowledge. Perhaps the Town Clerk knows something about it.'

'Yet a place like this . . .'

It stood out sharply: once, this had been an important house. The house of a mayor, or a lord of the manor – perhaps the most important house in Cross. Surely all record of it hadn't vanished except for the name of one forgotten owner?

'Perhaps you'll get on to the Town Clerk for me.'

'Yes, sir. Though I'm pretty sure there's nothing known about it.'

'Who'll have the deeds?'

Gissing thought. 'I believe Howard and Patch are the lawyers.'

He ignored the beleaguered front of the house and led Gently into the warehouse yard. The house apparently shared the yard because it was separated by no fence. A side-door opened directly into it, then came an outwork with grass-choked gutters, then an open-sided shed almost full of junk, and finally a high garden wall.

'That's the footway to Thingoe Road.'

A dim passage led away past the wall of the warehouse. Half a dozen kids who'd been chasing in the passage now clustered at the entry, watching the two policemen.

'A right of way?'

'Yes. That fellow's Colkett.'

A hard-framed man wearing a baize apron stood at the warehouse door, also watching.

'Did he see anything?'

'No. He packs up there at half-past five.'

'Did you talk to the kids?'

'One or two of them. But by then they'd all gone home.'

And that was that. By eight p.m. there would be nobody left in Frenze Street – perhaps not even a parked car farther down, at the town end. Just the old man living alone in his old, decaying house. With a door which, according to his nephew, didn't even possess a bolt.

And in one of his drawers, a fabulous medal. Why hadn't the murderer made a search?

'That door – the one that didn't lock – has it been secured since?'

'Yes, sir. We put a padlock on it.'

'Which is it?'

'This way, sir.'

Gissing led him into the open-sided shed, skirting several piles of rubbish. It was dank inside, and ferns grew on the house wall where rain dripped on it from the shed roof. Gissing struck a match. It revealed a cottage-type door with a simple latch-handle, but now fitted with a sturdy padlock which looked some centuries out of place.

Gissing unlocked it and pushed open the door. They went into a sort of hall or passage. At one end was a rusty gas-cooker and another door, which simply pushed open.

'The kitchen . . . I'd say he mostly lived in here.'

'What did he do about lights?'

'This . . . I reckon.'

Gissing pointed to a hurricane-lamp that stood on a concrete draining-slab near the door.

'Well – light it.'

The lamp made a squealing as Gissing hooked up the globe. A moment later its yellow light dimly showed them the low-ceilinged room.

A table, two deal chairs, a grandfather chair by the

old hobbed hearth. On the worn brick floor a strip of coconut matting. A brown-painted dresser with some bits of crockery. In one corner a door stood ajar to reveal twisty, naked backstairs. A third door led to an adjacent room. A fourth into a passage.

'Not much comfort in here.'

Only where the grandfather chair stood. The rest would be a wilderness of draughts, torturing the rheumatism in old bones.

'I reckon you'd need to be cracked, sir.'

Alone, with the winter nights passing. By a small fire with a dim light. The other one gone. Alone.

'Had he any money?'

'A few hundred quid, sir. All invested with a housing society.'

'And the medal.'

'Perhaps he didn't know its value.'

Or perhaps he didn't care. There was nothing left to buy.

'Let's see where you found him.'

Gissing took him down the passage, past a back hall with a fourth outer door, then to a front hall which ran the depth of the house and had two sets of stairs leading from it.

'Right there, sir. Where you're standing.'

They were at the foot of the inner stairs. A short set, they rose to a landing closed by a dark, panelled door.

'He was lying with his legs still up the stairs and his head twisted under a bit. Brinded, that's the milkman, came in for his money, looked up the passage and saw him there.'

'Did he move him?'

'Says he didn't. Not much doubt the old boy was dead.'

'Did you notice the expression on Peachment's face?'

'Yes, sir. Eyes open. Scared.'

And on the grimy floorboards, the bare stairs, no intelligible marks or footprints: not even much blood. A little had leaked from a broken bruise on the old man's cheek.

'Presumably he was attacked up the stairs?'

'Well, he did fall down them, sir.'

Though this was inference again. The appearance of a fall might have been faked.

'What's up there?'

'Just an empty room.'

'What was his purpose in an empty room?'

Gissing shook his head. 'That's a mystery, sir. Unless he went up there to hide.'

They went up the stairs. All they led to was an L-shaped room with a small window. It was not much larger than a big cupboard and was fitted with wide shelves in the toe of the L. They were made of thin, scrubbed, knotless boards, and suggested an old country-house pantry. A small deal table and a kitchen chair occupied a position by the window.

Gently pointed to the latter. 'These were here?'

'Yes, sir. Just where they are now.'

'You examined the shelves?'

'Yes, sir. No signs that anything had been removed.'

A strange room! How had it come to be worth a

separate flight of stairs? And why the chair and the table. What had old Peachment done up here?

If he'd been a writer, now . . .

Gently sat on the chair and rested his elbows on the table. Yes, that way round you could write at the table without your being in your own light. And then, on the table . . . He rubbed at a stain, held his finger to his nose, sniffed. Paraffin! The old man had stood his hurricane lamp on the table.

Gissing was staring around in his stolid way.

'I reckon he was hiding up here, sir,' he said. 'He could hear chummie moving around in the house, so he slid up here to be out of the way.'

'He could have locked himself in.'

Gently nodded to the door. It had an ancient lock framed into the panelling. Also it was fitted inside with a bolt, apparently of equal date with the rest. Lower down, a small panel was missing, leaving an aperture about the size of a postcard.

'Maybe he was too scared.'

Gently shrugged. 'Maybe. Was the door open when you found him?'

'Yes – and the key in the lock, the way it is now.'

Was it a sort of prison, that room? The door, for instance, was extremely solid. The window, which was the shape of a letter-box, had sockets in the frame that would take a bar. The floorboards were massive planks twelve or fourteen inches wide. Through the window you looked into an overgrown garden shut in by walls on three sides.

A prison . . . had there been a prisoner?

29

'Come on. Let's see the rest of the house.'

Suddenly he was feeling the chill damp of the place, the skin of his back was beginning to prickle.

'I tell you something, sir,' Gissing said, as they went down the stairs again. 'I wouldn't live here if someone paid me. I reckon this place has got too old.'

CHAPTER THREE

A PANTECHNICON RUMBLED by in the street and bumped into the yard with rattles and a clanking. Through cobwebbed lace curtains Gently could see some of the kids, huddled like starlings on the rail of a cattle pen.

Frenze Street.

He and Gissing had arrived in the book-room, a narrow chamber with a rotting floor and a mean little glazed-tile fireplace.

Not exactly a library! On the inner wall stood a black-painted bookcase about six feet high, shelves above and lockers below, and two drawers with brass ring-handles. A writing-table, a couple of chairs and a ragged carpet were the rest of the furniture. The floor had rotted through in a corner near the hearth. Everywhere dust, cobwebs, rot-smell.

No wonder Gissing hadn't lingered there in his hopeful quest for a blunt instrument.

'One of those drawers . . . ?'

There were no others. They each took one and

tipped its contents on the carpet. Old receipts, some twopenny almanacks, chalk, a thimble, a set of false teeth. In Gissing's drawer, a couple of farthings, one bearing Queen Victoria's head.

Was it credible that the medal had turned up amongst this rubbish?

The books, furry with dust, were sticking to the shelves and each other. They comprised a few cheap classics, books on horses and farriery, novels, a ten-volume county history. In the lockers below they found Peachment's old account-books along with more receipts and a family Bible. A quaint wall-cupboard under a window contained nothing but dry rot.

'I don't know, sir . . . it's hard to believe . . .'

Gissing lit a fag with grimy fingers.

From a long way off they could hear shouting and bumping as the pantechnicon discharged its load in the yard.

'You think young Peachment is trying to work something?'

'Well, sir, if he'd swiped that medal . . .'

'But someone did kill the old man.'

Gissing fanned smoke. Then slowly he shrugged his shoulders.

They packed the trash back in the drawers and left the book-room to its rot. But wherever you went in that icy house you met neglect and decay. Rooms that were furnished had been left to frowst behind closed doors and jammed windows. Empty rooms, showing wormy floorboards, exhaled a doggy smell that was unmistakable.

In a cheap wardrobe in one of the bedrooms they found a woman's clothes hanging, below them a hand-bag and mouldy shoes. On the dressing-table, a prayer-book.

'The lofts . . . they're worth seeing.'

Each loft was reached by a separate staircase. Three great halls under the high-pitched rafters, they suggested the carcases of long-dead whales. They were floored, and one possessed a huge hearth. The rafters caging them were rot-stained and peppered. A number had been replaced with poles of fir to which the bark was still clinging.

Then there was the priest-hole, or something like one, which Gissing had discovered in a downstairs room. The drawers below an alcove in a wall pulled out, and lo! behind them was a small, dank cell.

Where they'd hidden the gold?

Gently knelt and pushed his head in. Light filtered down from a small, high window. But the alcove could have been of later construction, and was probably only intended to fill an awkward corner.

And yet . . . one more odd thing about Harrisons.

'Let's go out into the garden.'

Gissing led him to a cobwebbed door that clearly had not been used lately.

From the rear, the house looked a planless jumble. The space between the wings had been filled carelessly. Grotesquely sloping auxiliary roofs made cradles for moss and even young saplings. Then, the west wing . . .

'Look . . . that wing is different.'

Standing out here, you could spot it at once. Besides

being taller, the west wing was brick, while the rest of the house was timber-framed.

'Older, would you say, sir?'

No doubt of that: the stone-framed windows gave it away. And above, badly in need of pointing, reared the original chimneys Gently had noticed.

'Listen . . . those curious features . . . they're all in this corner of the house. The priest-hole, the rooms at different levels – including the one where Peachment was attacked.'

'And now you see why. We've two different houses . . . the main part built on to something older. Sixteenth century – even fifteenth . . . perhaps going back to the Dissolution.'

'You mean . . . ?'

Gissing put on his blank look.

Gently shrugged and shook his head. At least it was something of a coincidence that an Innocent III medal had turned up here.

'Surely the house is on record somewhere.'

Gissing's blank look didn't falter.

'Isn't it scheduled?'

'Don't think so, sir. We've got so many old drums round Cross.'

Gently moved deeper into the grassy jungle. Every line of the house was telling the same story. Compare, for example, the firm outline of the west wing with the slight sag and tilt of its neighbour. And the stone-framed windows: three complete storeys, against only two elsewhere – with those at the lowest level bricked-up, turning a sunken room into a half-cellar.

A house that silently seethed with history.

And an old, muttering man shuffling about it.

Under some rotting floorboard, behind a loose brick . . . wasn't it possible . . . just possible?

'Reckon that's the window of the priest-hole, sir.'

Gissing's interest flickered for a moment.

'And up there . . . that'll be the little room. You can just see the back of the chair.'

A tiny window with fixed, mullioned panes, and once a stout bar behind them. A punishment cell . . . a monkish prison? With an observation shutter in the door?

The garden itself was entirely enclosed and accessible only from the house. A sizeable plot, it showed no sign that old Peachment had ever set foot there.

'What's the old brick place over by the wall?'

'Don't know, sir. But I can guess.'

Gissing was right. It was a Northshire two-holer. In that county, they built their privies with two seats.

When they came out of the house the pantechnicon had gone, leaving a raffle of tea-chests stacked in the yard. The warehouseman, Colkett, was busy with a trolley, but he rested the shafts as they came by.

'Found any treasures?'

'Should we have done?'

Colkett was aged around forty. He had a leathery face with deep lines and smirking, inquisitive grey eyes.

He wasn't put out by Gently's rebuff. He leant grinning against the trolley. Then he fetched a tab-end from behind his ear and lit it, grinning all the time.

35

'If what they say is right. Where there's muck there's money, you know. And I reckon there's plenty of muck in there. You two haven't come out with clean hands.'

True enough. The grime of Harrisons had a peculiarly clinging quality.

'Have you a wash-place?'

'There's a sink.'

'Perhaps you'll be kind enough to let us use it.'

'Do what you like,' Colkett said. 'I reckon the police are always the guv'nors.'

He led them through the open doors of the warehouse into a small but comfortable office. At one end was a sink equipped with a water-heater. Near it a kettle simmered on a gas-ring.

'Home comforts.'

Colkett squeezed aside to let the policemen go through.

'I was just going to brew up with my sandwiches. Perhaps you gents would like a cuppa?'

After the old house, a cheerful place. An oil convector stove was poppling in a corner. A girlie calendar hung on the wall above a table on which lay a thumbed, black stockbook.

'You work here alone?'

Gently lathered with carbolic under a stream of water that was stinging hot.

'All alone. That's the way I like it. Just one boss and his shadow.'

'You knew Peachment?'

'I knew him.' Colkett puffed on his tab-end. 'Not

36

to talk to – nobody did. But I'd see him ambling across the yard. "Hallo, Dad," I'd say. "How's the screwmatics?" And he'd sort of laugh and mumble something. You know what I think? He was deaf. Got his ears all bunged up with wax.'

'Laughed, did he?'

Gently felt for a towel. Colkett shoved one into his hand.

'Well . . . when I say laugh. Perhaps you'd call it a giggle. Miss him I do . . . old Peachey.'

Gently handed the towel on to Gissing and took his pipe out of his pocket. Colkett sprawled easily on a corner of the table, watching, the smirk lingering in his eyes.

Opposite the table a double window overlooked the yard and the wall behind it. Above the wall, the back of Harrisons, its dead windows staring blindly.

'Do they keep you busy?'

Colkett grinned again. 'Busy enough. It comes in patches.'

'Still . . . you're comfortable here.'

'I don't grumble. When there's nothing doing I can put my feet up.'

'And enjoy the view.'

Colkett was silent. He rubbed the tab-end out in a tin-lid.

Gently carefully lit his pipe and laid the match in the same lid.

'How much do you know about old Peachey?'

'I've told you. I saw him around in the yard.'

'How long have you worked here?'

'Three, four years.'

'Did you never ask him in for a cup of tea?'

'No.' Colkett stared hard. 'Well, he just wasn't like that. I can't say no more. Mr Gissing here, he'll tell you. The nevvy was the only one who could talk to him.'

'That's about the cut of it, sir,' Gissing said, pausing in the act of lighting a fag.

'Still, it seems strange . . .'

Colkett's smirk was gone. This wasn't playing fair, his expression said. Here he'd been, offering them hospitality, and now Gently had decided to play the heavy!

'Do you know the nephew?'

'Of course I know him. Used to drop in here every fortnight. He's all right. You can talk to Adrian. Had him in here many a time.'

'Did he talk about his uncle?'

'Well . . . yes.'

Gently puffed. 'Go on,' he said.

'Well – joked about him. That kind of thing. Dare say he didn't mean any harm.'

'What sort of jokes.'

'Just jokes. About the way he lived, what he wore. How he used to wash down in the kitchen. How he made tea in an old billy-can.'

'And he'd tell you about the house?'

'No. Why should he?'

'About what you'd find behind those windows?'

'I tell you—'

'And the door that was never bolted?'

'Look—'

Gently puffed. 'Yes?' he said.

Colkett was staring with real fear, his roughened hands grasping the edge of the table. He sent a scared little side-glance towards Gissing. The local man was watching with stolid attention.

But then Colkett's hands relaxed a little, his taut breathing became easier.

'All right, gents – you're cops. I know you have to put the boot in. It's all in the way of business, isn't it? Way you blokes make a living.'

'Did you know about the door?' Gently said.

'Go on – ask me! No offence.'

'So I'm asking.'

'Yes,' Colkett said. 'The nevvy asked me to keep an eye on it.'

He brewed the tea. He didn't seem to notice the steady silence in the little office. He smirked as he poured out in chipped cups to which dashes of tinned milk had been added.

'I reckon I'm auntie every day – never got married, you with me? Don't fancy settling down with a mawther. They're all right on the other side of the fence. You gents take sugar?'

He stirred it in himself. The result was strong, camp-fire tea. From a drawer in the table he took a snap-tin which contained sandwiches and a slice of cake.

'Cheers – and I hope you catches him!'

Was he somehow trying to put them in their place? He began on a sandwich with a noisy nonchalance, as though sure they knew better than to interrupt him.

Gently sipped a little tea, then put the cup by.

'So you kept an eye on the house,' he said.

'That's right,' Colkett said, through sandwich. 'You keep asking. I've nothing to hide.'

'You'd know Peachment's movements.'

'Of course I'd know them. He went up town every day. Mornings mostly, about eleven o'clock time. Sometimes in the afternoon.'

'And in the evening?'

'Wouldn't know, would I?'

Was that answer rather hurried?

'I close up here at five-thirty. You don't catch me hanging around after that.'

'You're never here later?'

'No. Never.'

'You never have a load arrive here late?'

'Well . . . no, not really late, I haven't. Not so's I'm kept here all hours of the night.'

'But that does happen – you're sometimes here later?'

'All right then, it does – once in a blue moon. But not the night they did old Peachey . . . look, I got time-sheets round here somewhere.'

'Not October 27th.'

'No. I'm telling you.' He was fumbling through a folder of dockets and receipts. 'Here – this is it. One load that day. Warmingers. Come in during the morning.'

'Let me see.'

Gently took the sheet.'

'And . . . on October 26th?'

'So what about October 26th? Didn't I say I was kept late sometimes?'

He snatched up a sandwich and bit a huge lump from it, his eyes glinting indignantly at Gently. Then he washed down the mouthful with a gulp of tea, making a deliberate sucking sound.

'You think I'm telling you lies, then?'

Gently shrugged. 'Did you see Peachment on the night of the 26th?'

'No, I didn't. I was too busy. They bust open a great big case of nuts and bolts.'

'You saw his light?' Gently stared through the window.

'Do you think I'm always gaping over there?'

'You'd have to see it,' Gently said. 'You're looking straight across at the house.'

'So maybe I did see it and didn't notice.'

'Did you?'

Colkett hung on for a moment.

'All right . . . I don't know! Will that suit you? It's a month ago since all this happened.'

'I think you did see it,' Gently said. 'It was up in that window. The little window.'

Colkett breathed quickly, the fear back in his eyes. His slack mouth hung a little open. He gulped suddenly: 'Look . . . stop trying to get at me! I didn't have nothing to do with old Peachey.'

'You've been in that house.'

'No – yes!'

'You know what's behind that particular window.'

'Yes – all right—'

'When were you in there?'

'The next day—'

'When?'

'When Brinded found him!'

Gissing cleared his throat apologetically. 'He did tell us that at the time, sir,' he said. 'Brinded came over here to use the phone, and Colkett went to take a look.'

'A look – that's all!'

Gently sucked on his pipe. 'Interesting. And you went up the stairs to the room.'

'So if I did—'

'Was the hurricane lamp there?'

Colkett stared at him. He was sweating.

'There wasn't no hurricane lamp in that room.'

It took Colkett some moments to decide on his answer. All the while his big hands were clenching and his dragging mouth on the twitch.

'I didn't shift nothing – I know better! I left everything how it was. Just having a look, that's all I was doing, and I tells Mr Gissing all about it.'

'And no sign of the hurricane lamp.'

'No! How many times do I have to say it? I don't know about Brinded, whether he moved it. But there wasn't no lamp when I got there.'

'Even more interesting,' Gently said. He looked at Gissing. 'Where was the lamp when you arrived?'

'Where it was just now, sir,' Gissing said. 'On that old drainer in the kitchen.'

'Did you test it for dabs?'

Gissing shrugged.

'You won't find none of mine on it!' Colkett burst out. 'I'm not saying I didn't touch nothing, but not the lamp. I never went near it.'

'Did Brinded mention it?'

'No, sir,' Gissing said. 'He said he didn't go up the stairs.'

Gently puffed a few times. 'Well . . . it may not be important.'

Colkett's hand jerked across his brow.

'But getting back to the 26th . . .'

Immediately, Colkett tensed again.

'You were here at this table, perhaps signing for delivery . . . wouldn't you have glanced across at the house?'

'Suppose I did . . .'

'Wasn't there a light?'

'Why should I notice if there was a light?'

'You couldn't miss it. The big dark house. Even a candle would show up.'

'Look, I've told you—'

'Yes or no?'

Colkett rocked his shoulders tormentedly.

'So I say yes – is that a crime?'

Gently shook his head. 'Not that I'm aware of.'

'So?' Colkett dashed at his brow again. 'What do you want to keep nagging me for? I'm trying to help you, that's what, you don't have to treat me like a criminal. I did see a light, now I think of it. Up in one of those far windows. And it's no good asking me which one, because you can't see that in the dark.'

'Thank you,' Gently said. 'Who else saw it?'

'What do you mean – who else?'

'Who else was in the yard that night – besides you and a couple of vanmen?'

For a moment he seemed to have struck oil again. Colkett hesitated, eyes frightened. But then he pulled himself round once more and gave a nervous little chuckle.

'You're trying to catch me out, aren't you? There wasn't nobody here but us. Just me and Bill Charlish and his mate – Norkett Transport. You ask them.'

Gently grunted. They were back on safe ground! But he made a note of the names of the two vanmen.

Colkett, after rallying his nerves with a second cup of strong tea, returned quickly to his ingratiating manner of earlier. He saw the two policemen to the warehouse door almost as though they were old friends.

'Coo! You certainly know how to put a bloke through it. I wouldn't want you gents on my barrow.'

'No doubt we'll see you again,' Gently told him mildly.

'Any time,' Colkett smirked. 'Any time.'

Out in the yard again, Gently halted. By the wall of Harrisons were standing two old packing-cases. He walked across to them and hoisted himself up: he found himself staring at the west-wing windows.

'Noticed these before?'

'Yes, sir,' Gissing said. 'They were standing there the morning we found Peachment.'

From the warehouse door Colkett was watching. But he wasn't smirking now.

CHAPTER FOUR

THE KIDS WERE clustered round Gently's car, trying to read the speedo and the rev-counter. There were nine of them, aged around ten or eleven, dressed in the slightly passé clothes of country children.

Their leader, who might have been twelve, wore a shabby claret windcheater. He stood arguing arrogantly about the speed of the Sceptre – one hundred and twenty at least: hadn't he read it somewhere?

When the others caught sight of Gently and Gissing they scattered suddenly towards the sale-ground, but the older boy stood pat, swaggering defiantly, hands in pockets.

His followers called him. 'Dinno . . . come on!'

Dinno wasn't going to budge. He dug his hands deeper in his pockets and stared fixedly at Gently as the latter came up.

'Your car, mister?' he jerked.

'My car,' Gently agreed.

'Tell us it'll do a hundred and twenty.'

'It might,' Gently said. 'With the wind behind it.'

'There y'are – I told them it would! That's a good car, that one.'

'I find it satisfactory,' Gently said.

'Yuh, a Humber. They're good cars.'

Feeling authorized now, Dinno swaggered round the Sceptre, his dark eyes appraising its lines and decorations. He was a good-looking youngster with a smooth, sallow face, and short-trimmed hair drab with grease.

Over by the cattle-pens his mates stood hesitant, alarmed by this bold encounter with policemen. Then they began stealing silently closer, as though feeling the protection of Dinno's audacity.

'Seen your picture in the papers, mister.'

Dinno came back to stand stiffly beside Gently.

'You're one of the big ones from Scotland Yard. You're going to find out who killed old Peachey.'

'You knew him?' Gently said.

'Course I knew him! Come past here to school every day. He'd got a hoard of gold in there, mister. That's why someone done him in.'

'What makes you think he had a hoard of gold?'

Behind the Sceptre were horrified faces. Dinno was really going too far – swanking like that to a couple of coppers!

'Stands to reason. Everyone knows it. There's a lot of gold hid in that old house. They wouldn't just kill old Peachey for nothing. He was a miser, that's what he was.'

'Did he show you any gold?'

'What, old Peachey?'

'A coin, perhaps?'

Dinno shook his head. 'Misers don't let on they've got any money. They just gloat over it when no one's looking.'

'Anyone here?'

Gently glanced at the others. They shook their heads and murmured negatively. A thoroughly blank-looking bunch of kids, some with mouths gaping stupidly.

'You want to know who we think done it?'

Dinno himself dropped his voice now.

'Who?'

Dinno came closer. 'Old Cokey,' he said. 'You mark my words. He's a bad 'un.'

'You mean Mr Colkett?'

Dinno nodded, big-eyed. 'Always after us lot, he is. A real bad 'un. Mark my words. You'll find out he's the one who done it.'

Gissing cleared his throat. 'That's enough, young Rix.'

'It's true,' Dinno said. 'Cross my heart.'

'It's true I'll be pinching you,' Gissing said, 'if I hear you've been spreading tales like that. Now run off to school.'

'But it's *true*.'

Gissing took a threatening stride forward.

'Dinno, come *on*!' called a pudding-faced boy, and there was a general rush for the safety of the sale-ground.

Dinno alone departed with dignity. Hands deep in his pockets, he stalked across Frenze Street. Then a distant whistle spoiled the act and sent him sprinting after his henchmen.

Gently grinned at Gissing. 'Colkett's character won't save him. I gather you know our young friend?'

'Rix,' Gissing said. 'His father's a dustman. We've had him on a drunk-and-disorderly.'

'What about Dinno?'

'Caught him scrumping apples. I laid into his backside.'

'Don't you have a juvenile court at Cross?'

Gissing looked blank.

'Well . . .' he said.

Gently took Gissing to lunch with him. The locals had booked him in at the George, a severally recommended hotel with a back view over the Mere. It was a comfortable, eighteenth-century inn built around a coach-yard paved with cobbles. Its public rooms were oak-panelled and had voluptuous moulded ceilings.

The food was solid. Gently ordered a roast, and it was served with dumplings in place of Yorkshire-pudding. The fruit salad was off, so he took the apple tart, and was appalled by the helping placed before him.

Gissing, undismayed, ate firmly and steadily through his choices. A solid man. The George's menu was doubtless devised for such as he.

'That should keep the damp out a bit!'

He wiped his mouth carefully when he'd finished. He accepted a Cognac with his coffee, probably under the impression that it was customary with moguls like Gently.

'You know, the more I think about this business . . .'

They'd carried the coffee into the lounge. A

somnolent room, it looked through tall windows down a slope of lawn to the pewter lake. At one end the manager's wife and a maid were struggling to pin up Christmas hangings, for the rest it was empty: the town clock had boomed three some minutes back.

'Unless it's the nephew – and that's a big if—

'You're beginning to think like friend Dinno?'

'No. Colkett has an alibi – at least, I'm sure – but anybody using that footway at night . . .'

'You mean, they could see into those windows?'

'Well . . . there are no curtains at the back. And anybody curious could get on the packing-cases, and take a look over the wall.'

Gently clipped a cigar and put a match to it.

'And what do you think they'd have seen?' he asked.

'There's that medal . . .'

'He must have held it up for them!'

'Well . . . I don't know. He could have done that.'

Gently puffed some big rings. 'Chummie sees the glint of gold, perhaps knows he has only the old man to deal with. So chummie breaks in, murders the old man, hides the medal in a drawer, calls it a night. Am I making sense?'

Gissing used his blank look. 'But if Peachment was beaten up . . . perhaps he'd hidden the medal.'

'Let's say that happened – Chummie beats up Peachment, who then falls down the stairs and is fatally injured. Chummie rushes out, too scared to make a search – but not too scared to return the hurricane to the kitchen! Also, he pauses to put out the flame, unless somebody refilled the lamp later.'

49

Gissing shook his head. 'Suppose the hurricane wasn't used . . .'

'Could you beat a man up in pitch darkness?'

'No . . . but some other light . . . say chummie had a torch.'

'What was Peachment doing in the dark in the first place?'

Gissing kept on shaking his head.

'We've got it the wrong way round,' Gently said. 'Chummie didn't break in and attack Peachment. When chummie broke in Peachment was out – that's why the hurricane was found in the kitchen.'

Gissing stared a moment. 'Yes . . . that fits.'

'It makes more sense. Chummie didn't plan a murder. He was after the medal, or whatever the attraction was, and slipped in there while Peachment was out. Then Peachment came back and caught him at it . . .' Gently hesitated, nostrilling cigar-smoke. 'But what happened then isn't quite so clear. All those queer bruises . . . how did he get them?'

'Some sort of struggle?'

Gently shrugged. 'More as though he'd just stood there, letting someone beat him. So many bruises . . . it must have taken time. And apparently no sign that he grappled with an assailant.'

Gissing gave a little shudder. 'A bit spookish, sir.'

Gently grinned. 'Poltergeists. They'd be an answer.'

'There was a case—' Gissing said.

Gently waved his cigar. 'Not yet. We'll come back to poltergeists when we've drawn a blank with the chummies. Now what have we got?' He puffed several times. 'We've a chummie who knows there's something worth pinching. Either he's the nephew, or he's an outsider who spotted that something through a window. He watches the house. On the evening of the 27th he sees Peachment leave the house. Chummie breaks in, presumably knowing about the door having no fastening. He doesn't search, because you found no sign of it, so he knows where to go for what he's after. And where he does go is a curious little room which we find empty except for a table and a chair. And yet he doesn't leave immediately with his loot. There's time for Peachment to come back and catch him. And he doesn't push Peachment aside and run for it – he beats Peachment up leisurely, eventually murdering him. Then he goes, we assume with the loot, leaving behind the medal which he apparently didn't know about.

'Plainly, chummie is someone who knew Peachment, and who had spent some time watching him.'

'Colkett, sir – when you put it like that.'

Gently nodded among his smoke-wreaths. 'Colkett is the man who stands out . . . but didn't you say he had an alibi?'

'Well, sir . . . I . . . I'm certain . . .'

Gissing stared unhappily at his empty coffee-cup. At times he gave the impression of dodging down inside himself, as though to consult some private notebook.

'What was his alibi?'

'Well . . . pubs mostly. He's got a couple of rooms over Hallet's, the greengrocers. He had tea with the Hallets – he meals with them – and went off out at half-past six. He was in the Grapes straight after that,

51

and later on he went to the Marquis. The Marquis is my pub. I saw him there. I can vouch for him myself from about eight-fifteen.'

'When did he leave the Grapes?'

'After eight, he says. It's only a step or two from the Marquis.'

'Any check on that?'

'They know him at the Grapes. They think he was there till about that time.'

'But they're not certain?'

Gissing shook his head at the coffee-cup.

'Would Colkett know you use the Marquis?'

'He could do, of course.'

'Is it far from Harrisons?'

Gissing looked wretched. 'About five minutes' walk.'

Gently issued a long stream of smoke. Not an alibi of much consequence! If Colkett were chummie he could have left the Grapes with time in hand to do the job. Then – a cunning move – he could go to the Marquis, and put himself under Gissing's eye. When, later, he came to account for his movements, the local man would feel disposed to accept the story.

'Perhaps we'd better check Colkett again.'

'Yes, sir. I'm sorry about that . . .'

'Not your fault. There's nothing against him except that he's Johnny-on-the-spot. Then I want the evening of the 26th covered – get on to the van-driver and his mate – see if their story checks with Colkett's, whether they noticed him watching the house. And finally, Peachment. We'd like to know if he habitually went

52

out at nights, especially if he were seen on the 27th. He may just have gone out for a packet of fags.'

Gently took some rank last puffs and squashed his cigar-butt in an ashtray.

'Me, I'll tackle the other end – what chummie pinched from the small room.'

Gissing looked puzzled. 'You don't think the medal—'

'I don't think chummie knew about the medal.'

'Then what—'

Gently punched Gissing's shoulder playfully. 'Come on! Let's go before it snows.'

But the snow was no jest. Outside in Water Street a light mizzle had turned to sleet, and already the afternoon was so dark that cars were using dimmed headlights. Well-muffled shoppers, heads lowered, jostled each other on the narrow pavements, or overflowed into the roadway to set brakelights adazzle.

Gissing paused to button his massive greatcoat before stepping out in the hurly-burly.

'I'll get back to the station then, sir, and put some men on those jobs.'

'Where are the lawyers – what were their names?'

'Howard and Patch. That's them over there.'

'I'll give them a look. They may be able to tell us a few things about Harrisons.'

Gissing shrugged very slightly before turning to bull his way up the pavement.

Howard and Patch possessed an ornate doorway surmounted by a carved head of Solon. A clerk admitted Gently to a carpetless office where a thin-featured man rose to greet him.

'Pleased to make your acquaintance. If we can be of any assistance . . .'

He couldn't, as it turned out, and for an unexpected reason.

'You see, it's the Church . . .'

On his desk he'd untied a suspiciously thin sheaf of papers. Now, as he shuffled them out, you could see they were all fairly modern.

'What has the Church got to do with it?'

'My dear sir, they used to own Harrisons. From about 1800, I seem to remember, till . . . ah! . . . September 1888. They bought it for a rectory, I imagine, when the previous house fell into decay. Then they built the present rectory in Rushton Road, and Harrisons was put up for auction.'

'So how does that affect the issue?'

The lawyer gave him a bleak smile. 'The Church has a habit, if I may so put it, of being a little *ex cathedra* in property matters. What they give you is a Declaration that the property has been held and enjoyed by a certain benefice, and this is to constitute your title: no acceptance, no sale. In our case, title commences on 16th September 1888.'

'But . . . there must have been earlier deeds?'

'You could, er, try the Diocesan Registrar.'

'Is it worth it?'

The lawyer sighed, then gave a brief shake of his head.

Nor could he add very much else. Peachment's father had been the original purchaser of Harrisons. A

54

bid of two hundred and seventy pounds had bought it in those golden days. The name? – no idea. The legend? – a contemptuous shrug. Peachment's affairs? – he had no affairs: they ended the day he retired from business.

Going out of the office, Gently turned for a second look at old Solon. The sleet was gathering on his curly hair and dripping like tears from his vacant eyes . . .

Gently turned up his collar and tramped away grumpily. Hardly an encouraging beginning! In anywhere but Cross a place like Harrisons would have a pedigree a yard long. But here – what was it Gissing had said? – they had so many 'old drums'. Tudor chimneys were cheap in Cross – and blessed draughty into the bargain!

At the bottom of Water Street he spotted a courtyard with a shop running down the side of it. Behind misty windows he could make out silverware and spreads of decorated china. Propped in the courtyard were several cartwheels, a bronze dolphin and a pair of urns, while a sign suspended above the door bore an inscription in spidery gothic.

Gently stared at the sign, then went in, setting a door-bell clamouring. He stepped into a long, low-ceilinged room lined with shelves of china, plate, brass and pewter. What looked like the case of a harpsichord had been panelled with glass and now did service as a counter: it was stuffed with a hotch-potch of smaller trinkets, snuff-boxes, stay-fasteners, vinaigrettes. The shop was heated with oil radiators, which made it smell like Colkett's office.

'Looking for me?'

A short, chubby man had entered silently from behind a curtain. He stood smiling cheerfully at Gently through a pair of rimless pince-nez.

'Mr Bressingham?'

'In person. Who are you – one of the trade?'

Gently's grumpy expression melted. 'Do I look like it?'

'No . . . you don't have the mark of Cain.'

He came forward. He was carrying a newspaper. He spread it open on the counter.

'Look . . . I have to know who you are! They've splurged you across the *Eastern Evening*. It is you, isn't it?'

Gently glanced distastefully at the big front-page photograph. It was ages old – probably taken when he'd been working on the Sawmills murders.

'Doesn't help the public image, does it?'

'Oh, my gosh.' Bressingham's eyes twinkled. 'They could publish a print of a monkey's backside if they'd give me all that free publicity. You're spoiled, you know. But what can I do for you? Nice bit of glass? A Sheffield salver?'

'I'd like your help with some stolen property.'

Bressingham's face fell. 'Shouldn't I have guessed it . . . !'

He acted an exaggerated Jewish shrug, displaying white hands with cone-shaped finger-tips. He had a curiously cherub-like face, plump and sallow, with small, sensuous lips.

'Well . . . it's nothing on the list. I was checking through that only this morning. And all I've bought today is some marcasite, and a couple of rubbishy Staffordshire figures.'

'How about coins?'

Bressingham cocked an eyebrow. 'Somebody knocked off something good?'

'Well?'

The chubby man shook his head. 'I've had nothing in here but bread-and-butter stuff. Regular customers – you know. Amateur dealers, the last one of them. It's a sort of fever that's going around, everyone checking their change for chips off the moon.'

'Any gold?'

Bressingham's eyebrow cocked again. 'You're not in here to count my sovereigns?'

'Antique gold.'

'Have a heart! Where would you find that stuff in Cross?'

'That's what I'm wondering,' Gently said. 'Do you have anything of the sort in stock?'

Bressingham clicked his tongue. 'I couldn't sell it. It's big-money stuff, for ace collectors. I look at it in Seaby's, of course, and roll the figures round my tongue. But here you've done a good day's work if you can flog a crown for seven-pound-ten. I once sold a bloke a George III guinea, for twenty-seven-ten. That's my highspot.'

'And nobody's ever offered you any?'

'Never.'

'Or shown it to you?'

Bressingham hesitated. He looked at Gently a little oddly, his blue eyes large behind the pince-nez.

'Yes,' he said. 'I'm beginning to get it. This is old Peachey we're talking about, isn't it?'

Gently nodded.

'Poor old Peachey – with the hoard of gold under his floorboards! Yes, once in a while he'd drop in here, just to wag his old chin – he fancied horse-brasses, you know, I learned a lot about them from him. And somebody saw him here, right? And of course, he was flogging me pieces of eight! That's what half of Cross would have thought if they'd twigged the old boy in here. And now you're following up to see if you can catch me with a chest of doubloons. Am I right?'

Gently said nothing.

'Oh, you'd make a dealer,' Bressingham said. 'But I am right. I know I'm right. So you may as well stop foxing.'

'So,' Gently said.

Bressingham looked impish. 'Suppose there is something in it,' he said. 'Not what the gossip is reading into it, but – well, just a spark under all that smoke?'

Gently stared.

Bressingham began nodding. 'About a fortnight before the old boy died. He came in here when the shop was empty and got something out of his fob pocket. "Tarma," he said – he was broad – "what do an objick like this fetch these days?" And he unwrapped the paper with his gnarled old fingers and laid the "objick" on the counter.'

'And it was?'

Bressingham kept nodding. 'A gold coin – just the one. But a real beauty, mind you. Currently, they're fetching seventy-five quid.'

CHAPTER FIVE

'SEVENTY-FIVE QUID!'
Gently couldn't quite keep the surprise out of his tone. Bressingham's blue eyes flickered interestedly for a moment, then he smilingly wagged his plump shoulders.

'So there are some better ones about?'

'Never mind that,' Gently growled. 'Are you sure about this one – that you got the value right?'

'My dear man.' Bressingham looked pained. 'Seventy-five is catalogue price. I reckoned I might make fifty of it. I offered old Peachey twenty-five. What with over-heads and slow turnover you have to calculate on fifty per cent. They always knock you down, anyway – all my customers are rogues.'

'Do you remember what it was?'

'Oh come, now! It was an Edward IV angel. Cross above arms on ship, rose, and St Michael spearing the Devil.'

'What condition?'

'Extremely Fine.'

'Isn't that the next condition to Mint?'

'Yes – a real collector's piece. Looked as though nobody had ever spent it.'

'And Peachment just brought it out of his pocket?'

Bressingham nodded. 'I'm not so green as I look either. But old Peachey – well, you couldn't suspect him! He wouldn't know what tea-leafing was about. Of course, I asked him where he'd got it, and he said he found it in an old box – a bit mysterious and giggly, you know, but that was how the old boy was. I reckoned he'd dug up a family heirloom, something his dad had put away. Anyhow, he didn't want to sell it, just to know what it would fetch.'

'Did he mention others?'

'No.' The flicker reappeared in Bressingham's eye.

'What was this one wrapped in?'

'A piece of blue paper – pretty old, I'd say. What we call rag-paper.'

'How old is that?'

'Not as old as the coin! Paper would be rather crude in 1480. This was the stuff you find used in old pamphlets, say eighteenth-century or a shade earlier.'

'Eighteenth-century . . .'

Bressingham shrugged faintly. Naturally, he was putting two and two together! If there were other coins involved beside the angel, then it was scarcely a question of family heirlooms . . .

'You say the shop was empty when Peachment came in.'

'Yes. And there was nobody in the courtyard.'

'Who else did you tell about the coin?'

'Well . . . the wife. But she wouldn't have mentioned it.

'You're sure that's all?'

Bressingham spread his hands. 'This is a confidential business. If I started blabbing about what people bring in here I would soon be without customers.'

'I see,' Gently said. 'So just you knew about the coin. And you left it like that, he didn't want to sell it. You didn't try to persuade him.'

'What was the use?'

'I don't know,' Gently said. 'But that doesn't sound like the dealers I've met. They'd have jollied the old boy, upped the price, asked what else he'd got to sell.'

'Yes, but look—'

'Then they'd have fixed a visit just to get their foot in the door. He might have had other treasures, mightn't he? Some he didn't value as much as the coin. So they'd be along there, getting into the house, laying out fivers on the table – giving him a silly price for some trifle to let him get the feel of the money.'

'All right – so it's done!'

'But not by you?'

'I'm not pretending I'm an angel.'

'You didn't fix to visit him one evening – say October 27th?'

The blue eyes behind the pince-nez swam a moment, tense, a quirk of fear. Around them the chubby face hooked into a scowl.

'I . . . I don't like this!' Bressingham said huskily. I don't like it at all.'

61

Gently stared, keeping the pressure on. Bressing-ham's sallowness had taken a pallor.

'I . . . I needn't have told you about that coin. I was trying to give you some help. Now you turn on me. I don't like it. Inspector Gissing wouldn't treat me like that.'

'I'm not Inspector Gissing,' Gently said.

'It isn't fair,' Bressingham said.

'Oh yes,' Gently said. 'A fair question. Did you fix that visit or not?'

'I didn't!'

'Can you prove it?'

Bressingham looked at him wildly.

'Say by showing you were somewhere else,' Gently said. 'An alibi. For the 27th.'

'An alibi . . . !' Colour came rushing back into Bressingham's cheeks. 'Of course – I'm a bloody fool! You scared me so much I couldn't think.'

'You do have an alibi?'

'My God I do. I was up in town on the 27th. It was the meeting of the Antique Dealers Guild. I wasn't back here till the small hours.'

'Proof?'

'Yes!' He turned quickly to a shelf on which was stacked a raffle of papers. Diving into them eagerly he pulled out a journal which had been folded back at a certain page. He smacked it on the counter before Gently.

'Look – a report of the meeting on October 27th – and yours truly mentioned by name! Proposed by Thomas Bressingham, that the sharing of stands shall be permitted at the Antique Fair. Isn't that proof?'

Gently glanced at the report. The meeting had begun at 7.30 p.m. Judging from the number of resolutions passed, it had probably maundered on till after eleven.

And Bressingham, shocked by the sudden stab of suspicion, nearly had to have this perfect alibi dragged from him.

'Yes . . . proof.' Gently grinned at Bressingham.

'You're a right bastard, aren't you?' Bressingham said gruffly. 'Suppose I couldn't have proved it?'

'I'd probably have believed you.'

'Yes – I'll bet!'

Gently kept grinning.

To smooth his ruffled feelings, Bressingham opened a small cabinet and poured two whiskies from a cut-glass decanter. One he pushed across the counter to Gently, at the same time giving him a reproachful look.

'Cheers! I still think you're a bastard – but I can see that perhaps it was necessary.'

'Cheers. Am I forgiven?'

Bressingham chuckled and wagged his shoulders.

They drank. Bressingham leaned against the shelves, staring out at the dark courtyard. Flurries of snow were skittering against the panes and chasing each other across the flagstones.

A woman, a hooded bundle of clothes, came briefly to the window to stare at some rings; then the snow won and she dodged away again, hugging a shaggy fur bag to her side.

Gently finished his drink.

'You still want to help me?'

Bressingham twinkled. 'Not sure that I do! But yes, I do – for old Peachey's sake. I'd like to help even the score for him.'

'Look . . . I'll put some cards on the table. Another coin has turned up in that house. It's a medal, actually, a papal medal, worth around fourteen hundred pounds.'

Bressingham whistled softly. 'Deep waters.'

'Yes – and this is what I find interesting. The medal is also medieval, also in Extremely Fine condition. In fact, another collector's piece, and only the fourth known example. The other three are accounted for. And there have been no thefts of coins lately.'

Bressingham took another nip from his glass. 'The dates may not mean very much,' he said. 'You get collectors specializing in a period – medieval gold, if you own enough oil-wells.'

'But . . . a collection.'

Bressingham nodded. 'It certainly begins to look that way. And if old Peachey had it, he'd have had it honestly, which points only to one thing. Is that the theory?'

'That's the theory.'

'My goodness . . . after all these years!'

'But is it credible?'

Bressingham emptied his glass, remained a few moments gazing at it.

'You've got me into a corner,' he said. 'I don't know what to say about that. Of course, it's possible. In troublesome times it was common to stash one's gelt under a floorboard.'

'Let's take one troublesome time,' Gently said. 'Was there any religious foundation at Cross?'

Bressingham nodded. 'A Benedictine house. But it was neither large nor rich.'

'Where was the site?'

'Don't think it's known, and I'm pretty well briefed in local history. At a guess I'd say it was close to the Mere. The monks usually built where fishing was handy.'

'No connection with Frenze Street?'

Bressingham shook his head. 'I think we can forget the monks,' he said. 'I know that Harrisons is ages old, but my dealer's nose says we're off the track.'

'Let's get to the house, then. What do you know about it?'

'Not very much,' Bressingham admitted. 'We have a Town Plan of 1742 which shows it having bigger grounds than it does now. They ran through to Thingoe Road in those days, mostly a plantation and some formal gardens. There's a sketch in the library, circa 1750, showing the house with a backing of beeches and conifers.'

'How did it get its name?'

'No mention of that anywhere. As a matter of fact, Harrison isn't an indigenous name in these parts. It doesn't occur in the town rolls, feet of fines or church registers – though the latter aren't much help. They only go back a couple of centuries.'

'So?'

Bressingham shrugged. 'It blew in from somewhere. Once upon a time there was a Harrison of Harrisons.'

'He must have made an impression.'

'It was perhaps just his being a foreigner. Cross is clannish enough today – the Lord knows what it was like then!'

Gently nodded. The solution was probable. Being a well-to-do 'foreigner' was enough to make a mark. And certainly (x) Harrison must have been well-to-do to buy the old place in its heyday. One could visualize it crisp and newly decorated with its screen of tall trees, its plentiful servants, who were no doubt housed in the amplitude of the lofts. And the formal gardens, requiring gardeners, and the carriage and horses with their quota . . . yes, he needed to have money, that mysterious foreigner with the name that had stuck.

He found Bressingham watching him quizzically.

'Look . . . this is a bit of cheek on my part . . . I've the curiosity of the devil. Have you searched the house yet?'

'Not a proper search.'

'Well . . . if you want a ferret. I mean, this is just my line of country. I really do have a nose for it, and I know the local domestic architecture backwards. If there's anything there, I'm sure to spot it.'

Gently shrugged. 'If there's anything there! The theory is that it grew some wings on the night when Peachment was pushed downstairs.'

'But you don't know that.'

'It's a fair guess.'

Bressingham's magnified eyes stared eagerly.

'Forgive me – but on present evidence, you can't be sure there was anything in the first place. There are these two pieces, that's all, the Edward angel and the medal. They may be part of a collection, or they may be a red herring.'

Gently chuckled. 'Well?'

'Well – we can do better than that. If we find a hiding place, at least we know there was something hidden to begin with.'

'And we might deduce something from the cache.'

'Exactly. You might find old Peachey's prints. And some more of that odd wrapping-paper – perhaps even with coin-impressions on it.'

Gently grinned broadly at the chubby little man. 'You've clearly missed your vocation,' he said.

'It's cheek, I know, but when you stop to think—'

'All right, I'm sold. When are you free?'

The snow had a blizzardy touch in it when Gently stepped out in the courtyard again. All day the weather had been slowly worsening and the temperature edging lower.

Tomorrow was December, and there was Christmas round the corner . . .

In town, the weather wouldn't notice so much; here, it was bleak like the open fields.

Gently shoved his way into a newsagent's for a copy of the paper Bressingham had shown him. A sulky-faced girl, who'd been cuddling a radiator, came forward reluctantly to serve him.

'*Eastern Evening News.*'

'They're all gone.'

Didn't his voice proclaim him a 'foreigner'?

'Give me a tin of Erinmore, then.'

She took his money without a word.

A little town, with winter closing on it: all foreigners go home.

Turning into the street, he was almost knocked down by boys racing coatless through the snow. He recognized Dinno. The youngster dodged him, bawling, 'When are y'going to pinch Cokey, mister?'

'Come back!' Gently called.

But Dinno laughed jeeringly and bolted on into the darkness. He heard them whooping and jeering in the distance till the scurrying wind swept the sound away.

A little town . . .

One felt a relief in pushing through the George's revolving door, exchanging suddenly the snowy night of Cross for the suave civility of a hotel. Here at least they welcomed foreigners, and were always glad to see them!

'Any calls for me?'

'No, sir, but . . .'

The manager's wife nodded towards the lounge. Through the swing doors Gently could see young Adrian Peachment sitting tensely beside a rather pretty girl.

Gently grunted. More hand-holding!

'Better send in tea for three.'

'Yes, sir.'

And she actually smiled as she took his snow-caked coat and hat . . .

When young Peachment talked he had a sort of jerk which might one day develop into a twitch. Jeanie

Norton, his girl-friend, was obviously smitten with him and watched him with intent, smiling earnestness.

'I thought since I was up this way – I'd better, well . . . report in, sir.'

Or, what was more likely, he had been persuaded to by the neat-featured Jeanie.

'Why? Your movements have not been restricted.'

'Oh no, sir. But I still thought—'

'Why are you up here?'

'To see Jeanie. We're . . . well, you know . . . I'm often up here.'

And here at Cross, along with his Jeanie, the provincial touch was even stronger. His military jacket notwithstanding, you knew you were talking to a native.

Lighting his pipe, Gently studied the young man. Had he been tempted to dismiss him too quickly? Adrian Peachment was certainly an easy answer to a number of puzzling questions. He, alone, had talked with the old man. He, alone, was familiar with the house. He would know his uncle's habits, too, better than any outside watcher. And his alibi? Give him half an hour – the p.m. estimate was not precise – stretch it a little, and he could still have been back in his flat by ten p.m.

But, on the other hand, if he were guilty, why had he come to Gently? Some sort of contorted cunning? A compulsion not to leave well alone?

'I thought that Jeanie . . . it's important, isn't it?'

Jeanie was looking at Gently and blushing.

'What about Jeanie?'

'Well, she can tell you . . . the time I left, I mean! On the evening Uncle was killed.'

So this was it! Young Peachment had been worrying about that alibi, perhaps realizing it wasn't quite watertight after all. Jeanie, determined not to be flustered, fixed her hazel eyes on Gently, sitting very straight, legs firmly folded, hands placed together on her lap.

'We . . . we'd had a row.'

'What sort of a row?'

The wrong question! Jeanie flinched slightly.

'It was . . . does it matter?'

'Oh, I think so. As Mr Peachment says, this is important.'

Jeanie shuffled her hands a little. 'All right, if you really have to know. It was about . . . well, the truth is . . . I suppose you'd call me a little old-fashioned.'

'He wanted you to sleep with him.'

'Yes . . . no! It wasn't quite so . . . not like that. He wanted me to spend a weekend in town – Christmas shopping. That's all.'

'Staying at his flat, of course?'

'Well . . . yes. But it didn't have to mean what you're thinking. And anyway . . . perhaps it's the way I've been brought up. I know everyone does it these days, but . . .'

An old-fashioned girl – she was quite charming! And she'd probably turn out to be a handful. Her voice had that little edge of righteousness that ought to have been a warning to Peachment. But perhaps he wanted to be dominated? There didn't seem a lot of buck there.

'When did the row happen?'

'In the afternoon. Adrian went to visit his uncle.

70

Then we drove out ... I don't know. Rattlesham Heath, I think it was.'

'Did you go with Adrian to his uncle's?'

'No. I waited in the car. Old Mr Peachment was queer about people, he didn't like them coming in the house.'

'So Adrian wasn't there very long?'

'No. About twenty minutes, I suppose.'

'More like quarter of an hour,' Adrian Peachment said. 'I . . . well, we never had much to talk about.'

Gently nodded. That was understandable. One could visualize long moments of helpless silence – the old man with nothing left to say, the young man despairing of saying anything. Yet Adrian had still persisted with these visits.

'What rooms did you go in?'

Adrian Peachment hesitated. 'The kitchen, I think . . . he was in the kitchen. Then . . . oh, yes, he took me up to the store-room. He didn't say why. He was like that.'

'Which is the store-room?'

'It's the room up the stairs.'

'You mean the stairs he fell down?'

Adrian Peachment stirred nervously. 'This was in the afternoon – three o'clock. It's got nothing to do—'

'But he took you into that room?'

Gently drew steadily on his pipe. Always, one came back to the room . . . Yet it was a room you could take in at a glance – no panels to tap, no suggestive features.

'Think back carefully. You were in that room. Tell me exactly what you saw in it.'

'Well . . . nothing.'

'Take your time. Go over the whole room in your mind.'

Adrian Peachment stared unhappily, giving now and then his little jerk.

'I'm sure . . . nothing! Uncle never used it. You see, it was upstairs . . . it wasn't convenient . . .'

'The chair. The table.'

'Yes, well . . . that was all.'

'How long had they been there?'

'I think . . . always! At least, the chair . . .'

'That was fresh?'

'I'm trying . . . yes. The chair wasn't there before.'

'And the shelves – go over those.'

The young man's hands were twisting together.

'Empty . . . I'm sure . . . quite empty.'

'Not even, say – *a twist of blue paper*?'

It meant nothing, Gently was certain. It just reduced Adrian Peachment to shaking his head. He was baffled. He simply didn't know why Gently was hammering him about this.

'All right, then. But your uncle said *something*, he didn't just lead you up there in silence.'

'No . . . I forget. You didn't know Uncle! He'd mutter away, pulling you along with him.'

'He said something to you about the old house.'

'Yes, but I don't remember where.'

'Wasn't it up there in the store-room?'

'Yes – it could have been. I don't remember!'

'He was such a vague old man,' Jeanie put in, loyally trying to relieve the pressure. 'You couldn't have a proper conversation with him. He didn't listen to what you said.'

72

'Why was that?'

'Why? I don't know.'

'I've heard it suggested he was deaf.'

'Deaf?'

She looked at Adrian Peachment, but he was too confused to do more than shake his head.

Their tea arrived. Jeanie poured for them with a firm, unhesitating hand. In this slightly more genial atmosphere Gently tidied up details of the alibi.

They'd gone out snogging, that was plain enough, and Adrian had pushed for something more satisfying. After all, she was wearing a modest little ring, and was due to become an Easter bride. He'd stayed for tea. Their evening programme had been a visit to the local flicks. She found she had a headache. Adrian had left. The time, she was sure, was seven p.m.

'You went to the car with him – saw him off?'

'No. But I watched him from the window.'

'Where do you live?'

'It's in Broome Road. He didn't have to go back through the town.'

Then a drive of nearly three hours . . . hadn't Gently checked it himself this morning? It had taken him two and a half from Finchley, never mind the grind between there and Kensington. If the times were right . . .

He looked keenly at Jeanie, who was eating toast with an elevated finger. She caught his eye and smiled dutifully. No, you really couldn't believe . . .

'How long have you known Colkett?'

Adrian Peachment started, letting his cup collide with his saucer.

'I don't think I know—'

'The fellow at the warehouse. He says you're quite a buddy of his.'

Flush-spots appeared in the young man's cheeks. 'I'm afraid I scarcely know him. A couple of times – once I drank some tea with him. I assure you he's no friend of mine.'

'Didn't you tell him to keep an eye on Harrisons?'

'I . . . yes, just for something to say! I mean, Uncle living alone like that, and not having any neighbours.'

'You didn't discuss your uncle?'

'Well, no . . . that is, only making conversation.'

Gently shrugged and didn't push it. Colkett, in any case, was a liar.

But then, just as they were leaving, with the embarrassment of young folk, the interview suddenly spilt some pay-dirt. Jeanie, putting on her scarf, remarked nervously, 'Well, one thing's certain. People knew about the coins.'

'Knew about them?'

'Oh, yes. The kids at school all knew. My brother Jackie came in one day and told us old Peachey was selling his gold.'

Gently went still. 'How did he know?'

'Kids' gossip.' Jeanie smiled complacently. 'Young Phil Bressingham heard his father talking about it. Mr Bressingham deals in coins.'

CHAPTER SIX

ONLY GISSING WAS in the office when Gently
arrived back at the station. He listened poker-
faced to Gently's account of the Edward IV angel and
Jeanie's remarks.

Gissing, you felt, was surprised at nothing: he met it
all with a dead bat. Behind the screen of his heavy
features he slowly absorbed, brooded, adjusted.

'I reckon that opens it up a bit, sir.'

Understatements like that were his daily bread.

'If the kids knew about it, it'd get around. Our
chummie could be just about anyone.'

Brilliant deduction! Gently sat on the desk and
grinned at the local man. The office was dreary, but it
was warm, a place to spin-out and mull-over com-
mon-places.

'I mean . . . even if it was just the one coin, the kids
would say it was a sackful. Then if one of our villains
got to hear about it . . . what about Bressingham
himself?'

'He has an alibi.'

Gissing nodded blankly. 'Not that Tom's ever given any trouble.'

'Who are your villains?'

'Well . . . I don't know. There's one or two I'll have a word with.'

Gissing himself had had a little luck. He'd visited a shop in Thingoe Road. A general store, it was where old Peachment had bought his paraffin and tobacco. On two evenings a week they opened late, and October 27th had been such an evening. Though he couldn't swear to the 27th, the shopkeeper was positive that Peachment had come in one evening that week. He'd bought some matches. Among the contents of Peachment's pockets had been a new box of Bryant & May.

Thingoe Road . . .

'He'd have gone by the footway.'

'Yes, sir. Slap past Colkett's office.'

'All the same . . . a bit risky. No way of telling how long he'd be gone.'

'If Colkett knew where to find the loot, sir, it wouldn't be very much of a risk. He could slip in there and out again before old Peachey could turn round.'

'But – he didn't.'

Gissing condescended to frown. 'No, sir. He must have struck a snag. Maybe it was the way we thought, after all, and he did knock Peachey about to make him talk.'

Gently struck a mean match.

'Let's forget about Colkett for a moment. Peachment goes out into Thingoe Road, and that's where chummie could have spotted him. Is it a busy place?'

'Middling busy. Council houses, a bit of traffic.'

'Kids?'

'They've got their quota.'

'So?'

Gently put the match to his pipe.

But Gissing, after a pause, dead-batted that one.

'I don't know, sir ... it's asking a lot. If someone spotted him in Thingoe Road, they'd see he was only going to the shop. Of course, we could do a house-to-house ...'

He let it linger in the air gloomily.

Gently shrugged. 'It may come to that.'

Gissing just let it die.

And so, of necessity, they were back with Colkett, their only glimmer of a suspect. Gissing had put a Detective Constable, Scole, on the chore of rechecking Colkett's alibi.

'He'll be in the Grapes now, chatting up a few of the regulars. I'm going round to the Marquis myself. If you'd care to come out for a jar, sir?'

Gently thanked him but declined – there was pheasant on the George's menu. From Gissing's manner you couldn't tell if he were disappointed or relieved.

'One other thing.'

'Yes, sir?'

'I'd like a chat with those kids some time.'

'Yes, sir. I'll round one or two of them up.'

Gently made a face.

'Not like that!'

★ ★ ★

But then, after all, he didn't get his pheasant peacefully, like a private citizen on his honest occasions. First there were reporters laying ambush in the George's foyer, and Gently knew better than to brush them aside without a statement.

'Mostly a routine check . . . nobody likes open verdicts. One of the relatives was in touch with the Yard, so they sent me along to make some motions.'

They listened carefully, with hard eyes, trying to catch him in a revealing phrase. No crime reporter worth his salt could quite believe that Gently was routine . . .

'Who was the relative?'

'Peachment's nephew.'

Rule one: always tell them what they'd find out anyway.

'Can you give us his address?'

Gently obliged. With luck, they'd go haring off to an empty flat in Grout Street, Kensington.

'You're treating this as murder?'

'Yes.'

'Have you a lead, sir?' (Politeness with that one!)

'No. We're treating it as murder for the purpose of the check, but it could equally well turn out to have been an accident. I'm here to make certain.'

Some jiffling and staring.

'What about this rumour that Peachment had found a hoard of gold?'

Gently shrugged smilingly. 'Put it in your story. But just between us, it hasn't turned up yet.'

An effective performance: they went away to the

phones half convinced there wasn't a big one here. The odds were they'd just leave a stringer hanging around, unless Adrian Peachment set their noses twitching again.

He washed and went down to dinner complacently, his office door mentally closed. But alack, when he'd barely begun on his minestrone, in walked Sir Daynes Broke.

'Hullo, you old war-horse!'

Who would have expected him, forty snowy miles from Merely? In fact, he'd been to a Regional Crime Squad conference at Eastwich and was taking in Gently on his way home.

'There's a good cross-route, y'know . . . don't have to bother going through Norchester. I called at the station to have a look at the medal. Oh, glory. My fingers are still itching.'

And of course he stayed to dinner, exerting all the consequence of a Chief Constable. The head waiter, wine-waiter and waitress hovered around him in a sort of ecstasy.

'This pheasant now . . . fresh, is it?'

'Oh no, sir. We hang them at least a week.'

'Ah, so you know what's what.'

They loved him. They couldn't have enough of him.

Through dinner he chatted gossip to Gently, who would sooner have concentrated on his food; then, hand on his elbow, he steered him into the lounge and to the best seats by the log fire.

'Now . . . how is it going?'

The George, you felt, had become Merely Manor when Sir Daynes walked in. Outside, in the very centre of the cobbled courtyard, would be standing his B1 Bentley with its discreet flag.

Gently gave him a résumé. He listened intently, interrupting only at the mention of Bressingham.

'Know the fellow. Bought a George III guinea off him. Twenty-seven ten, but I had to knock him down.'

'How much was he asking?'

'Thirty-five quid. What are you grinning at?'

Gently shrugged.

Again, when it came to the Edward IV angel, Sir Daynes was stirred into an exclamation.

'The old devil! I've wanted one for years. I wonder what else he had his hands on?'

In the end he sat back, staring into the fire, his grey, wiry eyebrows drawn in a frown.

'An odd sort of business . . .'

As though ensconced at his own hearth, he tossed a few fresh pieces from the wood-basket on to the blaze. 'Y'know . . . how shall I put it? . . . this has the feel of something unusual. Out here, now and then, a strange thing can happen. We're not quite twentieth-century in some ways.'

'Something supernatural?'

'Don't be an ass! Though I dare say we have a little mild witchcraft. If people are credulous it's possible to work on them – saw plenty of that out in Malaya. No, what I'm getting at . . .' He hunched his shoulders. 'Look, take incest – there's an example. Up in town you probably never come across a case, but we've got plenty in the villages. And nobody cares very much. It's been going on since the foundation. You cockneys marvel at your TV sex, but out here they wonder what the fuss is about.'

Gently nodded. 'So what you're saying . . . ?'

'I'm saying this case has got a smell. It may be a straightforward robbery with violence, but it could be something with a rum twist. So keep your eye roving, that's my tip . . . damn it, man, I'm trying to help you! I've got the feel of the place bred in me. I'm trying to let you use my nose.'

But the coins were what really interested Sir Daynes.

'If we could just turn up that collection!'

In his own mind he was obviously now certain that the Harrisons hoard was a fact.

'Only to have them through one's hands . . . pieces like that Innocent medal. I'd make the inventory myself, and the man isn't born who could hurry me. What are you doing about them?'

Gently had left instructions for the usual routine circularization. Dealers were requested to report any offers made them of valuable antique coins.

'He couldn't have got rid of them already?'

Gently smiled, shook his head. Seaby's had known nothing of any recent eruption of pieces of this class on the market.

At last Sir Daynes talked himself out and Gently saw him into the Bentley. The snow had stopped, but a stingy wind was still whirling the loose flakes. Above black, snow-laden gables a pallid moon chased in the

81

clouds, and nothing stirred in the street beyond the gateway. All you heard was the wind.

He slept well, and made no effort to get down early to breakfast. A tea-tray was brought him by a broad-faced country girl who smiled and lingered to pull his curtains.

'What's the weather like?'

'I don't know, sir. Reckon that don't get any warmer.'

Pulling the curtains had admitted a dirty dullness that offered no competition to his bedside lamp.

After a couple of cups he rang the police station, snuggling back into the sheets while he waited for a reply. He caught Gissing just coming in. The local man sounded breathless.

'Morning, sir . . . oof, it's a sharp one!'

Gently clicked his tongue sympathetically. 'Any luck last night?'

'Not where I went, sir. D.C. Scole has come up with something.'

D.C. Scole had met a man called Ringmer who remembered an incident that happened on 27 October. Ringmer had entered the WC of the Grapes preparatory to going in the pub for a drink. There he'd met Colkett, whom he knew. Colkett left the WC ahead of him. Afterwards he'd looked for Colkett in the Grapes, but hadn't been able to find him there. Time, estimated seven p.m. Ringmer remembered the date because that day he'd backed a winner.

'Interesting,' Gently murmured from his snug cavern.

'Yes, sir, it puts him an hour adrift. But I thought I'd talk to Ted Ringmer myself, just to make sure he'd got his facts straight. After that we can have a go at Colkett.'

'What is D.C. Scole doing now?'

'He's making inquiries about Peachment's movements.'

'Tell him to wrap up well,' Gently said.

He coaxed another cup from the pot, then consulted the directory for Bressingham's number. The ringing-tone sounded for nearly a minute before the antique-dealer answered.

'Yes . . . hallo?'

'Chief Superintendent Gently.'

'Good Lord! You get up earlier than I do.'

'I was thinking . . . this morning, if you're not too busy, perhaps we could go along to Harrisons.'

'I won't be busy – not in this weather. But give me an hour to thaw out.'

'If I pick you up at ten?'

'That's more civilized. I'm human by then.'

Gently hung up and revelled a few more moments in the bland cosiness of bed. But he could think of no more calls to make. He sighed, and slid his feet to the floor.

Bressingham's wife was waiting in the shop with him, and she presented a sharp contrast to her husband. Gypsy-featured, she was tall and lean, and wore a simple black dress with panache. In her ears she wore small gold rings, and other rings clustered on her long fingers.

'Meet Ursula . . . she's holding the fort for me. Actually, she's a better dealer than I am.'

Ursula Bressingham shook hands with Gently, giving him a slow, hard-eyed smile.

'Ursula's a diddeki,' Bressingham said proudly. 'That means she's half-way to being a gyppo. Anyone who can get the better of her should have his name put up in sovereigns.'

'Tom talks too much,' Ursula Bressingham said. Her black, glittering eyes remained fixed on Gently. 'But it's no use trying to spruce you, Superintendent. You were born under the same sign as myself.'

Bressingham chuckled. 'Let's go,' he said. 'Next, she'll be telling you the initial of your girl-friend.'

'It's B,' his wife said. 'And she's known a lot of sorrow. But that was all over two years ago.'

Gently shrugged. 'What about this business?'

Ursula Bressingham shook her head. 'Watch out for danger.'

'I usually do.'

'Don't laugh. It could come when you least expect it.'

She stood waving as the Sceptre rolled away, over sugary snow brown with grit. Bressingham, tucked up in a greatcoat and a huge knitted scarf, cocked his head and gave Gently a sly look.

'Was the initial right?'

Gently grunted. It was just over two years since he'd met Brenda Merryn.

Bressingham was grinning. 'It's mostly mind-reading,' he said. 'And a bit of guessing. She's good, is Ursula.'

Nobody had bothered to grit Frenze Street and there the Sceptre was ploughing through virgin snow. Snow quilted the dead herbage in front of Harrisons and had drifted in a slope against the front door.

'My God, it'll be cold in there.' Bressingham shivered.

On the roofs, snow overlapped the rotting barge-boards. Smoothing out detail, it emphasized strangely the stoop of the ridge and the lurch of the gables. Chimneys stood out harshly; in every window snow was packed hard against grimy panes.

'We go in at the back.'

Across at Colkett's office a light showed mistily behind steamed glass; then a hand wiped a patch in the steam and Colkett's face peered out at them.

'Wait!'

Gently threw up his arm, making Bressingham stagger a little.

'What's wrong?'

'Just keep back. Sometimes snow can tell a story.'

It told one here. From the warehouse and the foot-way numerous tracks crossed the yard, keeping, for the most part, in the same line, as people had followed in one another's footsteps. There was one diversion. A churned-up path led straight from the tracks to the Harrisons outhouse. It showed no footprints. Whoever had made it had kicked out the prints as he came back.

'Stay here, will you?'

Leaving Bressingham to shiver, Gently cautiously entered the outhouse. But the outhouse was floored with hard-trodden cinder-dirt which, in any case, was frozen. He came to the back door. The padlock was in place and there was no sign of attempted entry. If a prowler had been there he'd brought no tools . . . could it be he hadn't known about the padlock?

He went out again and examined the snow-track, trying to decide if it were lately made. In some of the hollows was a little blown snow, but dustings were still being scattered by the wind.

'Everything all right?' Bressingham asked, his teeth nittering.

Colkett, in the office, was watching each move. Gently stared back. Then he beckoned to Bressingham.

'Come on. I want some words with that fellow.'

Colkett met them at the warehouse side-door, a wary expression in his grey eyes. But he managed to throw on a smirk as he greeted them:

'Anything I can do for you gents?'

'Let's get inside,' Gently grunted. He pushed past Colkett into the office. Colkett followed, his smirk drooping, and Bressingham crammed himself in behind.

'Sit down,' Gently said to Colkett. 'Put your boots on the table.'

'But what—'

'Sit down and do as I say.'

Very unwillingly, Colkett sat down and hoisted his work-boots on the office table.

They were damp, and had the clean-picked look of footwear that had been through soft snow. But in the crook of a heel there was a trace of black mud. Gently took out his pen-knife and scraped off a sample.

'Here!' Colkett said. 'So what's all this?'

Gently held the mud up to the light. Cinder-dirt? A laboratory could tell him. Meanwhile, just black mud . . .

'Why did you go to the house this morning?'

'Why?' Colkett pulled his boots down sullenly. 'Who says I did?'

'This mud says so. And a test will soon prove it.'

Colkett stared stupidly at the scrape of mud.

'You're having me on, aren't you?' he said. 'I could've picked that up anywhere. You can't swear where I got it.'

'Very well. Hand me one of those envelopes.'

'Yes, but wait a minute!' Colkett said. 'Suppose I did go over to the house. You can't pinch me for doing that.'

'You did?'

'I might've done.'

'That's not an answer.'

Colkett's leathern face puckered.

'Well, if I did. What about that?'

'Why did you kick out your prints in the snow?'

'I . . . because . . .' He got up from the chair. 'Look, there ain't nothing funny about this! So I went to have a peek to see if all's well. I'm the sort of caretaker round here, aren't I?'

'And the prints?'

'They're nothing either! I just don't like people knowing my business. So that's about it. All above board. Why can't you come and ask me proper?'

Gently stared at the warehouseman for some

moments. Gissing, somewhere, was doing his double check with Ted Ringmer. Perhaps Gently had better hold his hand ... set Colkett up later, back at the station. He flicked the scraping of mud to the floor.

'In future, you can leave the caretaking to us.'

'Don't worry – I will!'

Gently nodded to Bressingham.

They went, leaving Colkett scowling after them.

CHAPTER SEVEN

A RED DISC patched the umberish sky in the
direction of the town, but above and around it
was a great weight of slaty cloud, swollen with snow.

'Don't I know these old drums,' Bressingham
chattered as Gently led him into the outhouse. 'Oh,
my gosh. And the stuff they're selling is always in an
unheated room. Can you imagine it? Trying to price
their old treasures with your breath coming like smoke.
And there's usually been trouble when they call you in.
Somebody dead, the old home breaking up.'

'So this'll be familiar,' Gently grunted.

'Only too familiar,' Bressingham sighed. 'I've seen
some things that would break your heart. I often come
away with a load of rubbish because I know darned
well they don't have a bean.'

But once in the house the antique-dealer perked up.
He stood rubbing his hands and looking about him
cheerfully.

'This isn't so bad – I'll bet there's some stuff here. I
reckon I could get my expenses out of this.'

'Never mind the junk,' Gently said.

'No . . . but it helps me to get my bearings. And young Peachment is bound to want to sell it, so I may as well give it a look in passing. That chair, now . . .'

He picked up old Peachment's chair, took it to the window and turned it bottom-up.

'That's a nice old chair . . . could be Mendlesham . . . bit of worm in the seat, but nothing to worry about.'

He set it down and looked at it, his head cocked to one side.

'I think I could spring fifty bob.'

'What's it worth to sell?'

Bressingham's blue eyes twinkled. 'About seventeen ten. But of course, they'd knock me down.'

Patiently, Gently filled his pipe and let Bressingham continue his probe of the kitchen. In turn the dealer valued an old faded-faced clock, a battered coal-scuttle and some plates from the dresser.

'But the chair's the best bit . . . I'd go to a fiver. Only don't let on to young Peachment.'

'Then can we get to business?'

'My dear old chap.' Bressingham dusted his hands. 'What do you think I've been doing while I was prowling?'

They went through into the dining-room, where the performance continued, and where Bressingham felt he could go a tenner on the table. But Gently noticed the dealer's eyes were everywhere and his pointed-tipped fingers touching and exploring. Once he stamped on the floor.

'There's some rot down there!'

'The boards haven't been interfered with lately.'

'No. You don't find much hidden under floors. It's the obvious place, and it's inconvenient.'

He felt deeply, however, into a wall-cupboard that had been excavated in the massive chimney-breast, panting a little as he fingered the crevices in search of a loose brick.

Coming into the book-room, he paused.

'Now that's a useful old country bookcase . . . I had one of those a few years back . . . got a good day's work out of it, too.'

Gently said nothing. Bressingham advanced on the bookcase rather like a boxer shaping up. His hands strayed over it casually for a moment, then came to rest on the drawers.

'Nothing in here, I'll be bound. First place you'd have looked.'

'We searched them.'

'Of course you did. But I think I'll just have them out.'

He withdrew the drawers carefully, not giving the contents a glance, then slipping a torch from his pocket he went down on his knees and shone the torch into the cavity.

'Ah . . . aha!'

He reached into the cavity and struggled with something at the back. After a deal of grunting one heard a sharp click, and he lifted out a section of the match-board lining.

'There. I was sure there'd be one.'

Attached to the lining was a flat box or compartment. But all it contained was old Peachment's army papers and some yellowing snapshots, presumably of his wife.

Brassingham stared at these relics glumly.

'That's the trouble with secret drawers. Nobody keeps anything worthwhile in them – it's been a life-time's disappointment.'

'Still, that compartment wouldn't have held many coins.'

'I'd settle for it, stuffed with Pope Innocent medals.'

He gave the interior of the bookcase another scrutiny, but the one secret compartment was all it possessed. Then he turned to the books and, surprisingly, brightened again. He stood gazing fondly, hands clasped behind his back.

'Look – horsy stuff. I can always sell it. The old boy's got all the classics here. And that's Armstrong's *History of Northshire* – it fetches twelve or fifteen these days.'

Gently puffed indulgently, giving Bressingham his head. He was beginning to understand his man. And, strangely, he noticed, in the dealer's hands, the most unlikely junk seemed to take on value. Was it Bressingham's enthusiasm, so naive and infectious, or just the reverent way he handled things? Difficult to say – but he had the touch: he could discover beauty among the ashes.

'A decent bit of calf . . . and it has the map.'

Already you were seeing those histories in a connoisseur's library.

'I'll bet young Peachment'll take fifty bob for them.'

When they came in, Gently wouldn't have offered five.

Bressingham asked few questions and Gently gave him no directions. The chubby man seemed to work on a rationale of his own. He rarely explored the whole of a room or went on tapping expeditions; often, he would simply stand somewhere in the centre and let his twinkling eyes rove about.

When they moved to the drawing-room he was soon on the scent.

'It's older here . . . a lot older! Look at the ceiling – they've raised the floor-level. Under here there'll be quite a cavity.'

But he ignored the floorboards and went straight to the corner where the alcove cupboard concealed the priest-hole. Gently watched. Bressingham opened the door, ran his hands down the shelves, pulled out the drawers.

'Aha! Ha, ha! You knew about this one?'

'We knew about it,' Gently said.

'But have you been down there?'

'Not yet. I got the impression it was fairly recent.'

'Oh, my Aunt Matilda!' Bressingham exclaimed. His fingers rippled over the door. 'Look at those hinges. Look at that panelling. They can't be later than seventeenth century.'

'And the drawers and the alcove?'

'Same date. Some naughty Papist put this lot in. And who'd be more likely to have Papal medals – and a reason for hiding them under the mat?'

Gently shrugged, staring into the hole. It looked so dank and inaccessible. If old Peachment had found his way in there it was long odds that he couldn't have got out again. You could see the damp-slime on the lower walls and on the floor, four feet below ground level.

'It's too obvious. You couldn't be in this house a day without finding that hole. No doubt it was useful to duck into temporarily, but any organized search would find it.'

'No, not so easily as that,' Bressingham objected. 'You wouldn't spot it so soon if the place was dressed right – lots of furniture, curtains, tapestries, and the shelves packed with china and knickknacks. Then the lining behind the drawers would be back in place – you need to be in the hole to do that – so even if some old Roundhead pulled a drawer out he'd find nothing suspicious behind it. Give these boys a little credit. They were brought up on Inigo Jones sets.'

Gently grinned. 'Notwithstanding Inigo! I was thinking of the property's subsequent owners. Even if the vendor didn't show off his priest-hole, the new occupier would soon find it.'

'What then?'

'He'd find what was in it.'

Bressingham touched the side of his buttony nose. 'He might, my friend, and he might not. Especially if he didn't know that something was there. Give me a hand down, will you?'

In spite of his rotund build Bressingham was active enough when it counted, and he quickly stripped off his coat and muffler, knelt, and inserted his feet in the drawer-well. Gently, also kneeling, grasped Bressingham's wrists, and the dealer energetically wriggled into the hole. He stayed a moment, scuffling with his feet, then nodded to Gently to let go.

'Oops! It's solid, but it's like a butter-slide.'

Gently handed him down a torch. Bressingham flashed it summarily about the floor then, more carefully, over the walls.

'It's undercut a bit here behind the chimney. Is there anything at this level on the other side?'

'Yes – a half-cellar.'

'Hmn . . . that fits. It would've been the dairy or something before they raised the floor level.'

But this obviously was not what Bressingham was seeking. He turned his attention to the nearer wall. Here he was hidden from Gently by the alcove cupboard, and only grunts and gasps marked his progress. At last he moved back into the field of vision.

'Blast.'

'Haven't you found whatever it is?'

'Yes, I've found it, but it's no go. Want to come down and have a look?'

With slight enthusiasm Gently squirmed through the gap and landed in the slime beside Bressingham. Bressingham flashed his torch on the inner wall, which was constructed of weeping bricks.

'So what am I looking at?'

'Look – here, and here. Half-bricks put in for no reason.' He jabbed a dirty finger in the slime and sketched out a vertical line. 'Then . . . two feet away . . . exactly the same thing. The original doorway.

Only the so-and-so has been bricked up since Will was a Shakespeare.'

'What else would you expect?'

'My dear chap!' Bressingham drummed on the bricks with his knuckles. 'Just behind these is the floor cavity. You could hide gold by the sackful in there.'

'But if there's no way in . . . ?'

'Not so fast. Remember that half-cellar you mentioned. And then there's always the drawing-room floor, though I shall be disappointed if it comes to that.'

Gently gave him a leg-up, then hauled himself after. He was growing a little tired of the priest-hole angle. If Peachment had found gold, it must have come to hand easily, and not involved the old man in gymnastics or hard labour. But Bressingham wasn't so soon discouraged. He insisted on rolling back the dusty carpet; board by board, he checked the drawing-room floor, crouching to his task like a plump Sherlock Holmes.

'Too many new boards,' he sighed at last. 'It was probably repaired in the last century. That means other people have been down in the floor cavity – though of course, they needn't have found what we think was there.'

'Also, no loose boards,' Gently said drily.

'There's still the half-cellar,' Bressingham said. 'I don't know . . . I could have sworn I was on to something. That priest-hole is wasted if it doesn't have a secret.'

They visited the half-cellar. It was a dangerous trap that simply opened off the end of the scullery. You went down half a dozen slippery stone steps and began skating about in a noisome gloom. Because the ceiling consisted of oversize oak boards Gently knew they were beneath the strange little storeroom, and he flashed his torch along the seams in the faint hope that they had trapped something significant. But they hadn't, and Bressingham was equally disappointed in his quest.

'Oh dear. I'm getting the feeling that I'm flogging a dead dickey.'

Gently shrugged. 'We're not through yet. Let's take a turn upstairs.'

Bressingham shook his head. 'Upstairs isn't so good. That's where you're more likely to have had structural changes. And the lofts, they're worst of all – people are always repairing the roofs.'

Once again, Gently gave no directions, leaving Bressingham to follow his nose. They passed the stairs to the storeroom. Bressingham glanced at them. He continued along the hall to the main staircase.

'Shall I predict something?'

'Fire away.'

'The principal bedroom will have a high ceiling. It'll be over the drawing-room, on the original level, and they can't have dropped the floor of the loft.'

'Does that mean something?'

Bressingham stopped to twinkle at him. 'Just giving my ego a boost,' he said. 'That business with the priest-hole knocked my confidence. I'm no bloody good when I've lost my bounce.'

Gently chuckled, and they moved on. Bressingham

was right about the bedroom. A lofty chamber, it had far more presence than the beetle-browed room below.

'Of course, the drawing-room was once like this . . . there was a bit of style about Tudor. Still harking back to the old halls with a fire in the middle and a hole for the smoke. Then timber-framing came in and it wasn't conducive to shapely rooms . . . and here we've got the two together. It's the rummest place I've ever poked round.'

Gently drew on his pipe. 'Tell me how it happened.'

Bressingham looked aslant. 'How do you mean?'

'Well . . . a Tudor wing, built, left unfinished, then completed in a later style.'

Bressingham stared silently for a moment.

'We're back with the monks again, aren't we?' he said.

'Both the coin and the medal are pre-Reformation.'

'Yes – only it needn't mean a thing.'

'Let's follow it through.'

Bressingham took out some Manikins, lit one, breathed pungent smoke in the icy air.

'All right,' he said. 'But it's pure theory. There isn't a trace of this in the record. We had a Benedictine cell – that's fact, and they were probably just as corrupt as their neighbours. So they were getting rich through flogging indulgences and defrauding heirs and other rackets. They've been living since the year dot in some old hovel by the Mere, but now they're getting delusions of grandeur and they've lost their taste for coarse fish anyway. Is that your idea?'

Gently nodded. Bressingham nosed a little smoke.

'They get their hands on a suitable plot – not by buying it, if I know them – and put some spiritual pressure on the local contractor to run them up a snazzy monastery. But when only one wing is finished Henry VIII cracks down on the priestcraft, and our holy friends get booted out, leaving their crock of gold behind them. Then . . .' Bressingham paused. 'Then I think there'd have been a lawsuit, perhaps between the contractor and the original copyholder. Result, delay; and so the reason why the rest of the house is in a later style.'

'Would that be plausible?'

'Oh, quite. Except perhaps for the crock of gold.'

'What's wrong with that?'

Bressingham winked slyly. 'I imagine the contractor would know where to look for it. But there's another reason – that scrap of blue paper. It fits too well with what we saw downstairs. There's a pong of seventeenth century round here. All the time I keep getting it.'

He flicked the ash from his Manikin and set off determinedly for the other bedrooms, but his rather cursory examination of them suggested that he wasn't finding the pong there. It was the same in the lofts, though they seemed to excite him by their size and odd perspectives; he spent some minutes squinting through gaps that revealed the whole run of the under-roofs. Finally, he gave his mock Jewish shrug.

'Well . . . let's get down to the *pièce de resistance*.'

'What would that be?'

Bressingham chuckled. 'I think we both know that, don't we? I noticed you watching me as we passed those stairs — and stairs were much mentioned at the inquest. Come on, stop foxing. We're two old pros. If we're going to crack this, we'll crack it together.'

Gently grinned broadly round his pipe.

'You, you old dealer,' Bressingham said.

They returned to the stairs. Following his usual procedure, Bressingham began by standing still and looking. Also, you felt, he was attuning himself, like a medium beaming in on some new vibrations. He flashed his torch up the stairs, letting it play on the walls, the landing. The storeroom door had been left ajar and the table and chair were partly visible.

'They found him at the foot here?'

'Where you're standing.'

Bressingham didn't bother to move. You could see his blue eyes calculating: the open door, the drop from the landing. 'What was he doing here?'

Gently hesitated. 'You'd better treat this as confidential. We think he came back from a short errand to find an intruder up in that room.'

'And he went up and tackled him?'

'That's the theory.'

'He was a braver man than I'd have been.'

'Unless,' Gently said, 'he knew the intruder, wasn't expecting any trouble.'

Bressingham looked at him, shrugged slowly.

'I don't like this place,' he said. 'The rest of the house feels pretty all right. Here it doesn't. You feel you're not wanted.'

'You mean there's a ghost?'

Bressingham didn't laugh. 'I see a lot of old places in my trade,' he said. 'Mostly they're friendly, sometimes not. This just strikes me as one of those places.'

He flicked the torch about again.

'Anyway,' he said, 'we're back on the trail. That door up there is the right century – probably coeval with the door of the cupboard.'

They mounted the stairs, and Bressingham's fingers were soon roaming over the door. The lock, the hinges, the bolt, the panelling all came in for a loving caress.

'I'll stick my neck out. I'm pretty certain that the same man was responsible for both these doors. There's a style about them. You can feel it in the bevelling. And the hinges came from the same blacksmith.'

'What about the aperture?'

'Ah. That's a puzzle.' Bressingham's fingers went lightly round it. 'It had a shutter, of course . . . a metal plate . . . with the missing piece of moulding attached to it. When it was in place you wouldn't know it was a shutter; it would look like a plate let into the door.'

'Any guesses?'

'Well . . . a Judas window?'

'Judas windows are usually higher up.'

'They are today,' Bressingham admitted. 'It might have been different when this was made.'

'But a Judas window . . . in a storeroom?'

Bressingham shook his head. 'I shall have to cogitate. They were rum old boys in the seventeenth century. Often you can't figure what made them tick.'

He turned his attention to the room, going first to

the shelves in the extension of the L. In the course of handling them, Gently noticed, he tested each one for looseness. Then he rapped the plain scrubbed panels which lined the walls in way of the shelves. Once he paused and repeated his raps, only to shrug faintly and continue.

'Was that anything?'

'I doubt it. Perhaps a crack in the wall or a missing brick. You can rip the place apart, of course, but nobody has ripped it apart lately.'

'Just . . . shelves.'

Bressingham nodded. 'A linen-store, to be precise. That's the reason why it's lined, to prevent the walls soiling the linen.'

'Is it the same date as the door?'

'Yes . . . which is rather puzzling. I've come across other stores like this, but never one guarded by such a door. I suppose . . .' He stepped over to the window. 'Yes, here we are – a barred window. So either Johnny had sheets of gold, or he amused himself by locking up the servants.'

'Have you noticed the bolt is inside the door?'

'Please,' Bressingham said. 'Don't confuse me. I'm beginning to get the ghost of a theory. Be a good fellow and let me think.'

Gently shrugged and relit his pipe. In his own mind he was sure they were drawing a blank. If there was a secret hiding-place somewhere in Harrisons it was not one which old Peachment could have stumbled on by accident. Nor were there signs that he had made a search, no jemmied floorboards or loose bricks; just undisturbed neglect on every side. Many rooms he probably hadn't entered for years.

But Bressingham probed on, with little grunts and buzzings, now playing his torch along a wall, now squatting down to inspect the floor. Eventually he returned to the door and checked if the key would work the lock from inside. Then he stood very still for some moments, the key held in his hand.

'I think I've got it.'

His eyes were sharp with excitement behind the thick pince-nez.

'There's only one thing all this adds up to – and that's a seventeenth-century orgy-room.'

'An orgy-room!'

'Yes – I'm certain. It would explain the door, and the bolt being inside. And the secret peep-hole at just that level – so that Johnny could spy on his pals from the landing.'

'But – why the shelves?'

'Camouflage. To make it look like an innocent store-room. Also, if the place is littered with bed-linen, who's going to notice the odd bed?'

Gently puffed hard. 'I suppose it's possible . . .'

'My dear sir, it's the only credible answer.'

'So then that Latin tag' – Gently nodded to the door – 'would you say it was something spicy from Petronius?'

Bressingham stared at the door. In the course of his checking he had pulled it wide open into the room, and now the outer side was lit by a pale snow-light from the window. The light had revealed lettering. In each of two upper panels were lines of small, embossed capitals. They were probably metal, but blackened by age, and one or two half worn away.

'Oh, my gosh!' Bressingham exclaimed.

'Can you read Latin?' Gently asked.

Bressingham shook his head. He was gazing at the letters in a sort of gap-mouthed stupefaction.

'Something about the gate of Olympus being difficult?'

'Heaven knows . . . don't ask me!'

'What's so surprising about them, then?'

Bressingham gulped. 'They're so . . . familiar.'

Inevitably, he had to touch the letters, like a blind man going over braille. Then he slipped a pen-knife from his pocket and gently scraped the patina from one of them.

'Lead . . .' He went on shaking his head.

'You've seen them before?'

'Yes – I'm sure of it. And they give me a queer sort of feeling, like I was walking into the past.'

'They read like a quotation.'

'But I don't know any Latin – not beyond *hic jacet* and *fid. def.* It's a visual thing . . . my memory's like that. Oh gosh, if only I could remember!'

He stood frowning fiercely at the letters, as though he could will them to give up their mystery. Then slowly he spelled them out, with an accent that was probably execrable.

'*Difficilis, cels* – four dashes! – *sera, porta, Olympi, . . . Fit, facilis, fidei, cardine, clave, manu.*'

'And it means nothing?'

'Nothing. Except that I must have seen it and taken notice of it.'

'Then perhaps it's to do with your business.'

Bressingham stared hopefully for a moment, then gave another shake of his head.

CHAPTER EIGHT

A ND THAT WAS it. All Bressingham's mental wrestling wouldn't recall the provenance of the Latin, though he promised to give the matter no rest until he succeeded in tracking it down. Of his identification of the store-room he remained positive, but that, alas, was academic. Orgy-room or linen-closet, it offered no key to Gently's problem. It was secure; probably it had no other connection with Peachment's treasure.

Bressingham felt his failure. He smoked a last, despondent Manikin with Gently. From the glum expression on his chubby face you might have thought he'd just lost on a deal.

'Well, anyway, we've debunked the legend.'

His hands, like Gissing's before him, were filthy. His neat bow-tie had got aslant and the tails of his muffler hung down to his knees.

'And yet, I'd swear old Peachey was honest. Anything else doesn't make sense. You just couldn't picture him doing a job, especially a big one that needed planning.'

Gently grunted. That was certainly out! If Peachment had been a regular villain, the police would have known about him. Collectors of gold coins didn't leave them around for casual sneak-thieves to pick up.

'Could they have been dumped on him?'

Yes . . . more likely. Though it still left a great deal to be explained. It argued that the thieves knew Peachment well enough to trust him, while by all accounts, except for his nephew . . .

Gently shrugged. 'We only know of the two pieces.'

'Oh, come now!' Immediately Bressingham perked up. 'Two pieces like that. You can trust my instinct. They're only the tip of a fabulous iceberg.'

'Then where did it come from?'

'Ah, that's your problem. But there's gold around and I can smell it. Perhaps I'm not so good as I think – you can always have a go at the floorboards.'

It was snowing again when they came out of the house, little dry flurries of small flakes. Across the yard the light was switched out and both doors closed. Gently checked momentarily. Bressingham glanced at him.

'Do you fancy that fellow . . . or shouldn't I ask?'

'You shouldn't ask,' Gently grunted. 'And I shouldn't tell you. Yes, we fancy him.'

'Ah,' Bressingham said. He was silent for a few steps, then: 'I don't like him much either. Once I had to chase him out of my courtyard. He was smooching there with a bit of jail-bait.'

'It doesn't make him a killer,' Gently shrugged. 'By the way, which school does your son go to?'

'Phil?' Bressingham looked his surprise. 'He goes to Cross Central. That's just over there, across the sale-ground.

He kept looking for Gently to explain his query, but Gently merely unlocked the Sceptre and got in.

At the station Gissing was back from his chat with Ted Ringmer. D.C. Scoles had also come in, and sat drinking cocoa along with his senior. Scoles was a lean, quick-eyed youngster. He quickly rustled up a mug of cocoa for Gently. For some minutes they drank and thawed silently, just three men who'd come in from the cold. Then Gissing drew his hand across his mouth.

'Don't know about Ringmer, sir,' he said.

'Oh,' Gently said.

Scoles, tipping his mug, looked anxiously over the rim at Gissing.

'His story checks all right, sir – same as he gave Jeff here – but I reckon he spent some time in the lounge before he went through to the bar to look for Colkett.'

'He told me a few minutes, sir,' Scoles said promptly.

'Yes,' Gissing said. 'He told me the same. Then he mentioned a conversation he'd had with the barmaid, about how his horse had come up at Thirsk.' Gissing paused to drink. 'So I checked,' he said. 'I went over to the Grapes and talked to Dolly. And she reckons he was talking to her in the lounge, for about half an hour, from around seven.'

'Was it the right evening?' Gently asked.

'It was the right horse,' Gissing said. 'Irish Wedding

in the four o'clock. That's what he says, that's what she says.'

'How does she estimate the time?'

'Well, with him drinking whisky,' Gissing said. 'Seems he got through two double scotches, which she puts down at about half an hour.'

Gently drank some cocoa. This had closed the gap again, though it still left Colkett with over half an hour – and, in fact, he might never have gone back into the Grapes after Ringmer had met him in the toilet. Thus, an hour and a quarter: time to watch, to enter, to kill – and time hastily to hide his loot, if he used the place that came handy. Search the warehouse? Gently pondered. All this had happened a month ago. Yet Colkett could scarcely have got rid of the goods, and he had nowhere but the warehouse to hide them.

'A pity,' Gissing said. 'We haven't got him nailed, sir. And I reckon we need to before we go after him.'

Yes: it remained suspicion. They had nothing material on Colkett . . . yet.

'What else have we got?' Gently asked.

Gissing tilted his mug towards D.C. Scoles. The young man flushed nervously and felt for his notebook – but didn't, Gently noticed, refer to it.

'Sir, first I visited Norkett Transport and spoke to William Charlish and Benjamin Tooke. They were the driver and mate of the pantechnicon that unloaded at Hampton's Warehouse on October 26th. They arrived there at ten minutes to six p.m. and left at twenty minutes to eight. Colkett had been advised there would be a late delivery. He was still on the premises when they left.'

'What was the load?' Gently asked.

'Mostly furniture, sir, and some small machine parts. They'd loaded the furniture at Southampton and picked up the other stuff at Slough.'

'What happened at the warehouse?'

'Just routine delivery, sir. Colkett was complaining at being kept late. He showed them where to put the stuff but didn't offer to lend them a hand. I gathered he was in the office most of the time, but they can't be positive about that. He was in the office when they finished because Charlish went there for his receipt.'

'And they left him there.'

'Yes, sir.'

'He wasn't standing by to lock up?'

'No, sir. They definitely left him there. There was still a light burning when they drove off.'

'Interesting,' Gently said. 'At first, he's complaining at being kept late. Then, nearly two hours later, he hangs about when he might be getting away. I wonder why.'

Scoles tried to look intelligent.

Gissing cleared his throat. 'Do you reckon he'd seen something?'

Gently nodded. 'I reckon he might have done. Especially remembering the view from the office window.' He drank cocoa. 'Did Charlish and Tooke see anyone in the yard?' he asked Scoles.

'No, sir, I did ask them. There were only some kids playing about.'

'Kids?'

'That's what they said, sir. I reckon they were kids

from Thingoe Road. They played around there and in the sale-ground – it sort of keeps them off the road, sir.'

'When did they see these kids playing about?'

Scoles flushed. 'Didn't exactly ask them, sir.'

'"Playing about" – was that the term used?'

'Yes, sir,' Scoles said defensively. 'Those very words.'

Gently stared at his mug for a moment, then shrugged. 'All right,' he said. 'Carry on.'

'That's all about Charlish and Tooke, sir. After that I made some more inquiries about Peachment's movements.'

The sum of these was small enough. Scoles had worked the areas adjacent to Frenze Street. About all he'd learned was that once in a while people had seen old Peachment out of an evening. On 26 October, nothing. On 27 October – perhaps – his visit to the shop. The latter had been a lucky strike in a blank which would probably now never be filled.

Gently added his own negative contribution of an account of the abortive search with Bressingham. Gissing listened with customary stolidness, a man who expected no gifts from fortune.

'I don't know . . .' He emptied his mug and set it heavily on the desk. 'I reckon we've got to nail Colkett, somehow.'

He caught Gently grinning. He looked perplexed.

The kids had made a slide, smoothing the snow into glassy marble. It was near the pig-pens, where no doubt an area of concrete underlay the snow. Whooping and screaming, they broke into a sprint and hurled themselves recklessly at the hard strip, some flying down it crouched, like speed skaters, others stiff-legged – or on bottoms and elbows. There were ten of them, going at it in a sort of wild group ecstasy. As each one skidded or blundered to a halt he turned and raced back to rejoin the queue. Their cheeks were flushed and their breath smoked, and their voices had a harsh, animal hoarseness. Almost they seemed to be acting a ritual, to be possessed by a snow-madness.

Then they noticed Gently, and the bubble burst. They drew together in a loose cluster. Still panting, they stared at him large-eyed, colts who'd been disturbed in their frolic.

'Don't stop for me,' Gently smiled.

But that was no use: the spell was broken. They kicked a little at the snow and stared aside from him sullenly.

He came up to them. They stood their ground, but cautious, ready for flight. Dinno was in the centre of the group. Alone, his steady gaze met Gently's.

'Well, Dinno,' Gently said.

Dinno's hands crept into his pockets. His shoulders pulled into a swagger. He was the leader. He knew it.

'See you got him then, mister,' he said.

'Oh?' Gently said. 'Who, Dinno?'

'Old Cokey. You took him away. It's all locked up – we been to look.'

'Yes, that's right, mister,' slurred the pudding-faced boy, who seemed to play the role of Dinno's lieutenant. 'Old Cokey's gone. We been to look.'

'You took him away,' Dinno repeated.

Gently shook his head smilingly. 'I expect he's gone to lunch,' he said.

'Oh, no he haven't,' Dinno said quickly. 'He's always there dinner-time. That's right, ain't it?'

'Yeh, yeh, that's right, mister,' the others chimed in.

''Cause we go there and cheek him,' Dinno said.

'He come out and chase us,' said the pudding-faced boy. 'Suffn mad he get with us, old Cokey.'

'Well,' Gently said, 'I haven't taken him. You'll no doubt find him back there tomorrow.'

'We was going to snowball him,' said the pudding-faced boy, regretfully.

Dinno stared at Gently with suspicion.

Gently took out his pipe and began to fill it. All of them watched his movements compulsively. There was a blank eagerness in their gaze as though they were witnessing an awesome mystery.

'So you see quite a lot of Colkett,' Gently said. 'I don't suppose you're always cheeking him.'

Dinno said nothing. The pudding-faced boy casually stubbed his toe in the snow.

'What's your name?' Gently asked the latter.

He squinted slightly and muttered: 'Moulton.'

'Moosh,' Dinno said.

'Which is Phil Bressingham?'

'Pills. He go home to dinner.'

Gently nodded and struck a match. Again it proved a wonderful event.

'Is he a pal of yours?'

Dinno said nothing.

'He's in our class, mister,' Moosh said. 'Pills don't come with us much. There's him an' Tubby an' Jacko Norton.'

'He's got some gyppo,' Dinno said disparagingly.

The others stirred their feet and sniggered.

'His ma's a witch. She's proper gyppo.'

'He int so bad,' Moosh said.

Gently puffed. 'He'd know a bit, wouldn't he? His father having deals with people.'

They thought about that one carefully, watching the smoke curl over his pipe.

'You see,' Gently said. 'It's like this. People knew about old Peachey's money. We want to know how they found out. I thought perhaps you could give me some help.' He indulged his audience with a small smoke-ring. 'Didn't young Pills say anything to you?'

They shuffled a bit and Moosh looked at Dinno. Dinno's hands worked in his pockets.

'Pills didn't tell us nothing,' he said. 'Nothing we didn't know, any rate.'

'But he told you something?'

''Bout old Peachey. He was selling some of his gold. Got a big old bag, he said. Full of gold. He was going to sell it.'

'A bag?'

''S what he said.'

'Tha's right, mister,' Moosh corroborated. 'Only I reckon Pills was making that up.'

'Course he was,' Dinno said. 'He's a lying gyppo.'

They stared righteously at Gently, that high-ranking punisher of untruths.

'Still, I expect you talked about it,' Gently smiled.

Again Moosh looked at Dinno for a cue.

'S'pose we did,' Dinno said carelessly. 'Only we knew about the gold. Always.'

'But you were only guessing before,' Gently said. 'Now you knew old Peachey had it.'

'We always knew.'

'But now one of you had seen it.'

Dinno worked some heel-marks in the snow.

'P'raps we kidded about it,' he said. 'Might've kidded a few people.'

'Kidded them how?'

Dinno gazed at the heel-marks. 'You know. Let on we'd seen old Peachey counting it.'

'And you had seen him?'

Dinno kept his heel stabbing. None of the others were making a sound.

'Just kidding,' Dinno said. 'Like we'd been watching him, seen him do it.'

'Watching through a window?'

'That's what we said.'

'Which window did you watch through?'

'We didn't. Not really.'

'Which window did you say?'

Dinno came down heavily. 'Just one at the back.'

Gently puffed. 'I see,' he said. Nobody was looking at him now. Most had their eyes fixed on the snow, a few stared vacuously about the sale-ground. Dinno's heel went on chopping out crescents, one placed close to another.

'This would be in the evening, wouldn't it?' Gently said.

''S what we told people,' Dinno said.

'You'd have been playing round the warehouse,' Gently said. 'You can see the back of the house from there. Of course there's a wall. How did you see over it?'

'You can see over it,' Dinno said.

'Not unless you stood on something.'

'Well . . . there's them old boxes,' Dinno said.

'Oh, yes,' Gently said. 'I remember. So you stood on the boxes and looked over. You'd be looking straight at that funny little window, the one all criss-crossed with bits of lead. But wouldn't old Peachey have drawn the curtains?'

'He ain't got no curtains at the back,' Dinno said.

'No curtains?'

Dinno dragged his heel.

'Tha's right, mister,' Moosh said. 'You can look straight in there.'

Gently nodded and smiled. 'Quite right. None of the back windows have curtains. And of course, it would be dark, so old Peachey would've had a light.'

'He's got an old hurricane,' Moosh said.

Dinno scuffed at the snow angrily.

'Well, you could see it,' Moosh said. 'On the table.'

'We seen him have a hurricane,' Dinno said. 'A hurricane.'

Gently puffed peaceably, letting smoke go in regular measures. At last Dinno stared up at him. He flinched a little, but held his gaze.

'How many of you were watching?' Gently asked.

Dinno didn't answer immediately. His hands were busy in his pockets again, working silently, two animals.

Moosh and the rest, following their leader, had also turned their eyes back to Gently. Like anxious birds they gazed at his face, helpless, mouths pulling apart.

'Me and Moosh. Goggy. Ringo. We all got up to have a look.'

'Who else was there?'

'Just us lot.'

'Who was in the yard?'

He hesitated. 'Nobody.'

'Tell me what you saw.'

'Old Peachey.' Dinno was staring very hard. 'He'd got his gold out. You could see it. He was having a gloat over his gold. Sort of a flat box thing that was in, we saw him putting it on the table. Then he was picking it up, gloating over it, holding it up near the light.'

'You could see what it was?'

'Course we could. It was a lot of gold coins.'

'A lot?'

'Ever so many, mister.'

'More than two?'

'Coo! More like a hundred.'

Gently looked round the group. 'Is this what you all saw?'

There was a murmur of assent.

'And what you were telling people you saw?'

They shuffled, their eyes drooping.

Gently let his pipe work again. Dinno's eyes were

still on him. Brown, steady eyes. Eyes that didn't give much away. Gently grinned at him suddenly.

'All right,' he said. 'When was all this?'

'Don't know what date, mister,' Dinno said. 'Reckon it was just before old Peachey was murdered.'

'It's important,' Gently said. 'See if you can remember. Was there a truck or something in the yard?'

'There was a big old van thing,' Moosh said. 'They come out afterwards and drove it off.'

'Afterwards?'

'Well, that was afterwards. After old Peachey put his light out.'

'It was a big old green van,' Dinno said. He wriggled his boot into the snow.

'So they'd been unloading?'

Dinno said nothing.

'And there was a light on in the office?'

'Yeh,' Moosh said. 'There was a light, mister. I reckon old Cokey was in there somewhere.'

Dinno kicked snow. 'But we never see him.' He stared at a spot below Gently's chin. 'But he could've been looking out, mister. He could've seen old Peachey too.'

'He couldn't see what you saw,' Gently said.

'He could've seen,' Dinno said.

'And he could've been told,' Gently said. 'Isn't that what happened after the van left?'

Moosh hung his head. Dinno stayed composed. He negligently swung at some more snow.

'P'raps,' he said. 'P'raps we kidded him. We're always kidding old Cokey.'

'I think he came out and questioned you.'

'He might've come out.'

'Suppose you tell me,' Gently said.

'All right,' Dinno said, his leg swinging. 'Suppose he come out and we told him.'

'What happened then?'

'Wasn't nothing happened. Old Cokey got up to have a look.'

'He dint see nothing though,' Moosh said.

'We packed it in, went home,' Dinno said.

Gently paused, still grinning. 'And the next night?' he said softly.

Moosh's eyes swung up, goggling. Dinno's eyes didn't waver.

'We wasn't playing round there the next night.'

'Sure?'

'Course.' Dinno sounded indignant.

'You weren't there, didn't see Colkett?'

'I'm telling you, mister. We went up the Sloes.'

'All of you?' Gently looked around. Nobody felt like meeting his eye.

'Tha's right, mister,' Moosh whined. 'We was up the Sloes along with some girls.'

'A pity,' Gently said.

Dinno ground his heel in. 'But he done it, mister. We know he done it.' He looked a little wistful. 'You ain't kidding us, mister – you hant got him locked away all the time?'

'I'm not kidding you,' Gently said. 'I'm just wondering if you're kidding me.'

Dinno's eyes stared. 'We couldn't kid you, mister.'

'No,' Gently smiled. 'Not for long.'

A whistle throbbed thinly. They started, colt-like, every head turned to the sound.

'Mister . . .'

Gently nodded. Then they were running. Not even Dinno had another glance for him.

Gently stood some moments longer, sucking now on a pipe gone cold; then turned and plodded out of the sale-ground and crossed the road to the ware-house.

There was still no light. He cupped his hands at the window. The dim office looked chill and drear. He went to the door and silently tried it. Locked. Nobody at home.

CHAPTER NINE

THE SNOW HADN'T really given up; by afternoon it was starting again – big, feathery, sauntering flakes that clung to one's clothes and laid quickly. You could see it teeming down from the clouds, racing when the wind caught it. Snow-gloom pressed on the little town. Already it had a cut-off feeling.

At the George Gently met the stringer, who sat playing patience in the hall lounge. He looked up hopefully when Gently entered, an elderly man with a sad, lined face.

'Anything for us, sir?'

Gently hadn't, but he felt sorry for the stringer and paused to chat with him. His name was Wemys. In the end, Gently fudged him up a plausible non-statement.

Not much, after twenty-four hours on the case!

Gently went into lunch broodingly. Apart from the medal they had no concrete evidence – and the medal itself was evidence of what? For the rest, surmise, suggestive circumstance and the dubious witness of children. Perhaps enough now to throw at Colkett, but not nearly enough if he failed to confess.

Frowningly, Gently cut short his lunch. Soon, they'd be waiting for the breaks. The case was depending too much on Colkett – somehow, it needed opening up. He rang the station. Gissing was out. D.C. Scoles had nothing to report. Leaving the Sceptre in the courtyard, Gently plunged out in the snow again.

In Playford Road, off Water Street, he found the greengrocer's, Hallet's. It was open-fronted and looking miserable with snow collecting on the stacked vegetables. A woman minded it. She was stout and freckled and wore a shabby coat over layers of sweaters. There were no customers. She gazed at the snow with a sort of meditative spite.

'Mrs Hallet?'

'That's me.'

'Police. I want a word with your lodger.'

'Him.' She sounded withering. 'He's up at the warehouse. Won't be in till half five.'

'You haven't seen him?'

'Not since breakfast. If he's been back I haven't noticed.'

'Which are his rooms?'

'Over the top here. There's some stairs round the corner.'

They were iron stairs, running from a yard to a small landing at first-floor level. Snow lay virgin on the treads. Nobody answered Gently's knock.

'Told you so.' Mrs Hallet had waddled out to watch Gently. 'Up at the warehouse is where you'll find him. You know the warehouse?'

'I know it.'

She didn't ask him what Colkett had done, simply stared as he trudged away.

But she was a liar. Colkett wasn't at the warehouse, and snow covered the tracks leading to the door. Clearly he hadn't returned since he left while Gently and Bressingham were searching Harrisons. So where was he? Holed-up at some friend's? It wasn't a day to be tramping around. Had Gently scared him so much that morning that he'd decided to make himself scarce?

Gently shrugged grumpily, standing ankle-deep in the darkening yard with the white flakes whirling. Harrisons, the warehouse, both deserted; only the wind to make a little moan.

He went down the passage, where the snow was thinner, and emerged in Thingoe Road. This was livelier. A few cars were passing, their tyre-sound muffled, wipers sweeping. Almost opposite the passage was the general shop where Peachment had bought the box of matches. Its windows glowed yellowy against the snow and were filled untidily with tins and cut-outs.

Gently crossed over and entered the shop. It smelled of soap and dog-biscuits. Behind the counter a neat, grey-haired man was checking groceries into a carton. A couple of shelves were stocked with cigarettes and a few cheap brands of tobacco; below them, a shelf of matches. A sign said: *Aladdin Pink*.

'Police.'

The man glanced at Gently but went on checking, his lips moving. Then he scribbled on a piece of paper and stuck the pencil behind his ear.

'Yes? I'm a little deaf.'

To establish an entente, Gently bought tobacco. The grocer's name was Wix. He went through his story readily enough.

'What makes you remember Mr Peachment coming in?'

'Well, you see, it was the last time. The next I heard they'd found the body – rather upset me, that did.'

'Was that the next day?'

'I can't be certain. I wouldn't want to tell you a lie.'

'The 27th was a Thursday.'

'Tuesdays and Thursdays. Those are the nights I stay open.'

Gently put his questions slowly, giving Wix time to think. Almost certainly Wix had been the last but one to see Peachment alive.

'Did Mr Peachment often come in of an evening?'

'Well, now and then. When he wanted something.'

'I'd like you to tell me about that last time. Everything that happened, what was said.'

Wix did his best. He stared at the door, imagining Peachment coming in, then his shuffle up to the counter, his mutter, his request for the box of matches. It signified nothing. It was such a transaction as might have happened any time over the years. Nothing to say, when the doorbell pinged, that never again would it ping for old Peachment.

'Were there other customers in the shop?'

Wix shook his head. 'Not as I remember it.'

'Do you know Colkett from the warehouse?'

'I know him.'

'Did you see him that night?'

'I don't think so.'

'Who else was about here?'

'Well . . . customers. They come from the council estate mostly.'

'Kids?'

'Always plenty of them.'

'But do you remember them?'

Wix shook his head.

And, of course, the tobacco would be dry and unsmokable: Gently could tell it by the feel of the packet.

He left the shop and set himself doggedly to plod the length of Thingoe Road. Setting Colkett aside, this was the likeliest area from which Peachment's killer might have come. Gently had studied a map; the foot-way and Frenze Street offered a short cut to the town centre; and Peachment, Gently was certain, had known his killer by sight – as he would have known the regulars from Thingoe Road.

A long, a dreary road! The Council had widened it before they built. One side were huddled old town houses, facing them the bastilles of Council terraces. Regular culs-de-sac divided the terraces, bearing names like Councillor Bunwell Close and Hotblack Grove; in the dark and the snow the estate wore the aspect of a Siberian penal settlement. No wonder the kids played in the sale-ground, or got their kicks cheeking old Cokey.

On the town side many of the properties were doubtless marked for demolition. Adjacent to the warehouse was a terrace of cottages, their windows boarded, crosses painted on the doors. Gently crunched across to examine them more closely. They probably backed on the garden of Harrisons. Something possible there? He eyed their blankness for a moment, then hunched his shoulders and turned away.

A waste of time! Yet he continued stubbornly, up one side of the road and down the other. He wanted the feel of the bleak thoroughfare, of the people who lived there, who used that short cut. Council tenants, some near the breadline, a few already known to the police, going daily past the house where, according to the kids . . .

But the snow beat him at last. Numbed, he turned back towards the footway. In two lengths of Thingoe Road he had met scarcely a dozen pedestrians. Now it was truly dark, in place of the twilight of the snow-gloom, with flakes pitching down in sackfuls so that you couldn't see past the next street-light. He entered the footway. A shape moved ahead of him, going towards the warehouse door. Gently sprinted. The figure turned suddenly, flashing a torch. It was D.C. Scoles.

'Oh . . . you sir!'

'Me,' Gently said. 'You won't find Colkett in there.'

'Do you know where he is, sir?'

'Hasn't he come home yet?'

'No, sir. That's where I've just come from.'

'What's the flap then?'

Scoles hesitated. 'I thought you'd have been informed, sir,' he said. 'We've had a message from

Norchester. A man like Colkett sold a coin there today.'

Gissing was on the phone when they entered the office, his face as empty of expression as ever.

'Yes, sir . . . we'd like them today.'

He was arranging search-warrants for Colkett's and the warehouse. He hung up.

'You didn't find him?'

'No, sir,' Scoles said. 'He isn't back yet.'

'We can wait,' Gissing said. He looked at Gently. 'Reckon we've nailed him now, sir,' he said flatly.

It had begun to look like it. The jeweller in Norchester had given a good description of his customer: around forty, about five feet seven, grey eyes, lined face, strong local accent. The jeweller, named Deacon, hadn't been too suspicious when the man offered him the coin: since collecting coins had become a vogue all sorts of people brought him valuable pieces. His suspicions had been further set at rest because the man dickered about the price, and had spent half an hour nudging Deacon towards his ultimate bid of forty-five pounds. Only after he'd gone did Deacon consult his police bulletin.

And the coin? An Edward IV angel, wrapped in crumpled blue paper.

'It's on its way here,' Gissing said. 'Deacon paid for it in fivers. We just pick Colkett up with the fivers on him and I reckon that'll be that.'

'Do we know how he's travelling?' Gently asked.

'No,' Gissing said. 'But he doesn't own a car. I've

127

checked with the station. They don't remember him buying a ticket. I've put D.C. Abbots on meeting the train.'

'What about buses?'

'I've rung Broome. The local constable will board the bus there.'

'And if he's hitched a lift?'

Gissing nodded comfortably. 'P.C. Metcalfe is waiting at Hallet's.'

All earths blocked. And at the other end, Norchester, the CID would be covering too. Unless Colkett faded into the snow en route they'd have to have him before much longer. The break had come. The case was made – Colkett had been panicked into doing something stupid.

Or was it going to be quite so simple . . . ?

'Why did he sell that particular coin?'

Gissing stared, considering the question. 'I don't know . . . perhaps it was handy.'

'But just that coin – the one we know about – if he had a lot to choose from? And why just one? Why not several? He could have sold them to different dealers.'

'Perhaps he has done, sir,' Scoles said. 'Perhaps the other dealers haven't come clean.'

'Then we have to swallow that the one honest dealer was the one who bought the identifiable coin.'

Scoles shook his head, abashed.

'Perhaps he only had that one coin,' Gissing said heavily.

Gently nodded. 'And suppose he came by it honestly – or at least, without murdering Peachment to get it?'

'I don't see how—'

'Look,' Gently said. 'Peachment had been carrying that coin in his pocket. In his waistcoat pocket, Bressingham says, just loose, wrapped up in the piece of paper. So it could have shaken out when Peachment fell, and being wrapped in blue paper, it wouldn't show up. So the murderer could have missed it. And the milkman could have missed it. It could have been there for Colkett to find.'

Gissing stared unhappily. 'So what you're saying—'

'I'm saying Colkett probably wasn't the murderer. But if he was, then all he stole was the one coin off Peachment's body.'

It was perverse! Gissing gazed at his desk with the injured look of a sick goldfish. The very clincher that should have 'nailed' Colkett was being twisted into a defence! You could almost see Gissing's mind wrestling as he grappled with this naughty argument. Scoles, too, gone suddenly stiff, was clearly trying to find a counter.

'But it doesn't follow—'

'If it wasn't Colkett, sir—'

The two of them came in together. Colkett was chummie, and Cross CID wasn't letting him go without a struggle.

'Wait,' Gently said. He gave them a résumé of his talk with Dinno and the kids. They listened impatiently. A couple of times Gissing's lips shaped to interrupt. At last he exclaimed, 'But that's plain proof, sir! It proves Colkett knew what Peachment had got.'

Gently grinned. 'If we believe the kids.'

Gissing gaped. 'They couldn't've made all that up.'

'I put in some check questions,' Gently admitted. 'I

129

think maybe sometimes Dinno was leading me. But if it's true, then there was more than one coin – and it's long odds that one coin is all Colkett had.'

'But that's still surmise, sir!' Scoles broke in.

Gently shrugged. 'It's all surmise. We'll know a bit more when we pull in Colkett. One thing's sure – he'll have to talk now.'

Gissing was shaking his head bereftly, his eyes miserable and unseeing.

'I don't know . . .'

He had to believe! Within was pure certainty that Colkett was guilty.

'We'll search, then.' He rose blunderingly. 'Those warrants'll be across any minute. If we can just find the rest of those coins . . . they've got to be there. We'll find them.'

'And if they aren't?'

Gissing made a gesture, as though warning Gently to get behind him. He grabbed the phone and raked off a number.

Gently shrugged again, and pulled out his pipe.

The warrants came. In a stone-cold Wolseley they bumbled through the snows to Playford Road. Hallet's was shuttered, but a window down the yard spilled dim light on the foot of the stairs. Half a snowman, walking out of a doorway, proved to be Police Constable Metcalfe. He had nothing to tell them. After he'd told it he moved stiffly back into the doorway. Then a door opened cautiously in the yard and a thick-set, sweatered man peered out.

130

'Who are you lot then?'

It was Mr Hallet, with his plump wife peering spite-fully over his shoulder.

'You got a warrant, have you?'

Gissing flashed it at him. Hallet made him hold it closer to the light.

'These are my premises . . . what's up with old Cokey? You fare to want him rare bad.'

'When did you see him last?'

'Breakfast, I reckon . . . what's the trouble?'

Gissing didn't answer.

They clumped and kicked their way up the stairs. Scoles brought out a bunch of keys. The second one did it. They entered a chill atmosphere of bacon-grease and gas. Gissing, flicking a torch around, could find no light-switch, only a gas-bracket with a round, dirty glass. He hesitated, then struck a match. The lamp lit with a pop. Gissing seemed surprised.

'Mod cons, sir,' Scoles ventured.

Gissing grunted, staring around him. It was a smallish room with dadoed walls, cream above, dark green below. It contained an obsolete gas-stove and a chipped sink, a table, chairs and kitchen cabinet. At one end stood a painted cupboard. Pin-ups were taped along the walls.

Not much of a place to call home . . . yet it had a sort of sluttish cosiness. A gas-fire was fitted, and near it was wedged an old easy-chair, a newspaper lying on it. No TV, but a cheap radio, and a pile of paperback pornography on the cupboard.

Sometimes, you felt, Colkett put his feet up and gave the pubs a miss for the evening.

Did he bring a woman back?

Gently shoved open the door that led from the kitchen to the room behind. Another gas-bracket! Gently lit it. It revealed a room that was a twin of the other. A double bed, none too clean, and with a solitary, soiled pillow. A big, old-fashioned wardrobe. Painted chest-of-drawers. A varnished dressing-table jammed across the window. More pin-ups were plastered over the walls and, facing the bed, an obscene drawing. The room smelt doggy. If women came here they were rough ones, soused with drink.

A lonely man, that was Colkett. His job at the warehouse would exactly suit him. Aloof, probably friendless, inviting nobody up to his grubby retreat. A bit of pub company, some inept fumbling, then back to the sanctuary over Hallet's. Then, with pop music blaring, the sexual fantasies that stayed a dream.

A killer? Possibly . . . but it'd be a woman. In a panic, he'd try to talk his way out.

Gently went back into the kitchen.

'Having any luck?'

Gissing and Scoles were exploring the cupboard. Out of it had come a medley of rubbish but also a stack of small orange-and-black cartons. They contained car light-bulbs.

'Pinched,' Gissing said. 'He's been knocking these off from the warehouse.'

Gently shrugged. Every trade had its perks. Colkett probably wasn't getting very fat out of those.

He moved around the kitchen carefully. Really, it offered very little concealment. The cupboard, the cabinet, the easy chair, the cooker and possibly the case of the radio. He tried the chair. It had a loose seat-cushion. He felt around in the fluff beneath it. Two halfpennies, sixpence, a bent nailfile and evidence of addiction to liquorice allsorts. The rest of the chair was honest stuffing. The radio and cooker were equally innocent. Scoles, foraging in the cabinet, found a box of tyre-levers, but they were obviously loot and not tools of a trade.

'How about the floor, sir?'

They stared at the floor. It was covered with lino which had been tacked down. Gissing stooped and fumbled half-heartedly at a join, then suddenly seemed to remember they hadn't dealt with the bedroom.

Gently stood by the door watching, sure now that the search would be a frost. Colkett was a thief, that's all they were learning – a thief who perhaps stole for quasi-sexual thrills. A little man . . . a little thief. If he'd known about the gold, would he have dared to steal it? No . . . that single coin was more Colkett's mark, grabbed up off the floor when no eye was on him.

In the wardrobe Gissing found a new steelyard, and beneath the bed a case of spanners. Under the pillow was hidden a notebook. Scoles opened it and blushed. *Eskimo Nell* . . .

Hallet was lurking in his doorway when they came down the steps again. He looked sharply to see if they were carrying anything. Then he whistled a bar of Colonel Bogey. Gissing stopped.

'Where's the bog?'

'The bog?' Hallet gaped. 'Can't you wait, then?'

'The bog that Colkett uses,' Gissing said patiently. Hallet leered and pointed across the yard.

Scoles was assigned to search the bog: Gently and Gissing returned to the Wolseley. Gissing lumped down heavily in the driving-seat, shoved a fag in his mouth and lit it. He breathed smoke wearily.

'So it'll be the warehouse.'

'You'll need more men,' Gently shrugged.

Already, he noticed, he was opting out of an exercise he judged to be futile. He wanted Colkett . . . oh yes! – but he was no longer reckoning him as a possible killer. Vital now was what Colkett knew, not what they might turn up at the warehouse.

'There's D.C. Abbots . . .'

'You can't spare him. Grabbing Colkett is first priority.'

'Colkett's got to come back here.'

'He could spot the constable. And don't forget he's flush with cash.'

Gissing breathed more smoke, slow, tired, no doubt with the warehouse before his eyes. One might strike lucky, say in the office, but other than that . . . it would need an army.

'It's this bloody snow . . .'

'Leave it till morning.'

'I don't know . . . I still think . . .'

'Let's talk to Colkett. That's what matters.'

Gissing sat silent, just the smoke going.

CHAPTER TEN

THE SNOW WON. They drove back to the office along streets as empty as streets of a ghost-town. In effect the snow had eased, but it was lying now so thick that the Wolseley's wheels were continually spinning. Above, a black sky pressed heavily, suggesting the break was only temporary. Plenty more up there! By morning, Cross would probably be beleaguered.

At the office two messages were waiting. They came from D.C. Abbotts and the Broome constable – Colkett wasn't on the evening train, and the Norchester bus had failed to arrive. The Broome constable had done some phoning and had located the bus at Tattishall Crossroads. It was stuck in a drift. Its twenty-one passengers were being given shakedowns in Tattishall school. The constable had talked to his colleague at Tattishall and had passed on a description of Colkett.

Gissing rang Tattishall. No go – they didn't have a passenger resembling Colkett. He rang the railway station. There was one more train. As far as they knew, the line was clear.

Gissing hung up and gloomed for some moments.

'Reckon he's painting the town,' Scoles said. 'All that dough. It's burning his pocket. Reckon he'll come back juiced, on the eleven.'

'Suppose he picked up a tart . . .'

'Not him,' Scoles said. 'He's one of those blokes who'd be scared of a Judy.'

'If he knows we're after him . . .'

'How could he know, sir?'

Gissing shook his head. 'But I wish we'd got him.'

Gently hung on for another hour, then hunger drove him back to the George. Colkett would turn up. He wasn't a professional who knew how to vanish into the scenery. He could have thumbed a lift and got stuck, or merely have decided to stay in Norchester. Some transport doss-house . . . perhaps, at that moment, he was stuffing himself with egg and chips.

It was too late for dinner, but the manager's wife fixed Gently up with a plate of stew. At ten p.m. Sir Daynes rang to get his bulletin from Gently.

'Was going to call in – but this bloody snow! Had to pinch a Land Rover to get home.'

Then, at 11.10, Gissing. Colkett hadn't been on the train.

Not on the train; nor, apparently, in any hotel or doss-house in Norchester. Gissing, who'd stayed on the job all night, met Gently in the morning with bruised-looking eyes.

Norchester had checked. There was no hair of Colkett. Nobody had seen him since he'd sold the coin. They'd kept a man on the station and another on the buses, but no Colkett. The snow had swallowed him.

'Hmn,' Gently said. 'And he hasn't been home.'

'No.'

'Then he's probably stuck in the snow.'

'I've been ringing all night, sir.'

'That wouldn't find him. Not if he spent the night in a vehicle.'

Gissing drank glumly from a mug of cocoa, tiredness oozing from his sagging body. He'd let Scoles go. The young man, fresh, stood staring concernedly at his senior.

'The trouble is . . . we're cut off. They reckon the ploughs won't shift it today.'

'So – we'll have to be patient.'

'But all the time . . .'

He shrugged and dipped again into the mug.

Gently echoed the shrug. Where was the hurry? If Colkett was stuck, he couldn't be running. And probably the first person to reach him would be a village bobby, with Colkett's description. Nothing to do now but wait.

'You'd better take a spell,' he said.

Gissing stared at him, puffy-eyed. 'There's still the warehouse.'

'Give me some men. I'll look it over.'

Gissing hesitated, then shook his head. 'I'd sooner do it myself, sir,' he said. 'I've got some ideas . . . that stuff he was pinching. It's up to us to look into that.'

137

Colkett was *his* chummie, that's what he was saying. Gently had stopped taking Colkett seriously. It might even be he would skimp the job of taking apart those daunting premises. Gently grinned.

'Before you go, I'd like a run-down of your Thingoe Road clients.'

'Thingoe Road . . .'

'My hunch. Just in case we *don't* nail Colkett.'

The list was disappointingly short. Over the last five years there'd been little trouble in Thingoe Road – two embezzlements, some minor housebreaking, one g.b.h., twelve domestic disputes. A semi-habitual named Betts lived at 37, Brewster Drive, but he was currently doing a twelve-month stretch for receiving a stolen vehicle. Of the minor offenders only three had jobs which took them into the town centre, and one of those had been questioned by Scoles and could be more or less eliminated.

'Any thoughts about these?'

They hadn't; Gently pocketed the list and rose to go. But as he reached the door the phone went and he hung on to hear the message.

'For you . . . Tom Bressingham.'

Gently took the phone from Gissing.

'Hullo?'

'Superintendent? Listen . . . I've just solved your problem!'

'Which one?'

'All of them!' Bressingham gave a breathless little chuckle. 'And do you know something? The answer was in the house – all the time.'

★ ★ ★

Bressingham couldn't wait for Gently: he came up Water Street looking for him. They met amid the clanging of snow-shovels where a gang was excavating the narrow thoroughfare. Bressingham was rosy-cheeked and puffing. He hadn't bothered to put on a coat. Chuckling and gasping, he staggered up to Gently, arms held out as though to embrace him.

'Oh, my gosh. This beats everything. I've just stepped back two hundred years!'

'Hold it!' Gently laughed. 'What have you dis-covered?'

'Everything. The house – the legend – the coins.'

'The coins?'

'Yes. I can name you a couple of them. And the storeroom – I know all about that!'

'But how?'

'Aha! Ha, ha! Oh, my dear fellow, it's an absolute masterpiece!'

He grabbed Gently's arm and began dragging him down Water Street, through snow that was lying shin-deep. The sweating roadmen leaned on their shovels to stare amazement at the capering dealer.

'But the coins – this is fact?'

'Yes! Yes! Oh gosh, they'll be worth a king's ransom!'

'Look, tell me one thing—'

'No, not a word. This you *have* to see for yourself!'

They plunged into drifted snow in the shop's courtyard and at last were stamping outside the door. Ursula Bressingham opened it to them. Her black eyes were smiling at her bubbling husband.

139

'Come in, Superintendent. Tom's a little bit fey.'

'Good gosh, who wouldn't be?' Bressingham chortled.

'Tom, you're soaked.'

'Oh, woman!' – he danced impatiently into the shop.

Ursula Bressingham dropped the latch, then accompanied them through the curtain at the back of the shop. They entered a pleasant, well lighted sitting-room with windows looking out on the mere. It was quietly furnished with modest antiques and had a big china-cabinet on the back wall. In the centre was an oval pedestal table with two calf-bound volumes lying on it. Bressingham danced to the table.

'First, a little lecture.'

'Please!' Gently pleaded. 'Just give me the facts.'

'My dear fellow, you'd never appreciate them – not without knowing the whyfores first. Have you heard of Blomefield?'

'No.'

'Allow me to present the reverend gent.'

He picked up the larger of the two books from the table, ran his palm down the spine, then handed it to Gently.

'There – Vol One of the first edition – Fersfield, 1739. *An Essay towards a Topographical History of Northshire. Completed by Parkin*, 1775.'

'And this mentions Harrisons?'

'Ha. Aha! No – that's the point. It doesn't mention it.'

Gently groaned. 'So what am I doing with it?'

'Just getting some facts,' Bressingham gurgled.

'You'd better sit down, Superintendent,' Ursula Bressingham said. 'Tom isn't going to let you off lightly. This is his big moment. He really has uncovered something. I'll go and make a pot of coffee.'

She swept out, with her strangely regal carriage, and Tom Bressingham darted to place a chair for Gently. Gently sighed and sat down. What did it matter? His other business that morning was scarcely urgent.

Bressingham pulled up a chair to face Gently's, sat, and beamed at the detective for a moment.

'Now, Francis Blomefield. He was Vicar of Fersfield, that's a village a few miles out. His book is a classic – everyone wants it. I could sell this copy for a hundred quid.'

'Not to me,' Gently grunted.

'No, you old philistine!' Bressingham chucked. 'But if you lived in Northshire, or your family had lived here, then you'd be bidding me for the Blomefield. It's quite fabulous. It covers every parish – records, pedigrees, inscriptions, brasses. As far as I know it has only one drawback – it's about as readable as last year's Bradshaw.'

'Spare me the literary criticism,' Gently said.

'No, that's what I can't do.' Bressingham grinned. 'It all turns on that. It's because Blomefield was boring that another gentleman tried his hand.'

He picked up the second book and caressed it like the first.

'An eighteenth-century popularizer,' he said. 'His notion was to give a résumé of Blomefield, plus some interesting tit-bits and current comment. The same carucates and frank-pledge stuff, and quotes from Domesday by the bucket – but along with snappy pars about invasion defences, fairs, water frolics and local characters. Easily outsold Blomefield of course, and consequently he's not too scarce today.'

'And you want to sell me one?' Gently said.

Bressingham twinkled at him, shaking his head.

'But you could try young Peachment,' he said. 'He's got a copy. Only don't offer him more than fifty bob.'

Gently went still.

'That's right,' Bressingham nodded. 'Ten vols. Armstrong's *History of Northshire*. And I noticed Vol Two didn't have any fluff on it.'

He handed the second book to Gently.

'Vol Two,' he said.

'Am I interrupting?' Ursula Bressingham said, coming back just then with a tray.

Bressingham giggled. 'The Super's just got the scent. I could leave it with him now, and he'd soon have the answer.'

'In here,' Gently said.

'In there. One of Mr Armstrong's gossipy asides. Look up Cross, under *Cross Hundred* – I'm not going to spoil it by giving you the page reference.'

'Tom, you're a tease,' Ursula Bressingham said. 'I'm sure the Superintendent is a very busy man.'

'Oh, but not too busy for this,' Bressingham giggled. 'I want him to have the full, fantastic flavour.'

Ursula Bressingham set down her tray and poured coffee from a pot which was probably white Worcester.

Gently opened the book. It was laboriously printed on a fibrous laid paper, beginning to fox. It covered four hundreds or county divisions: Clavering, Depwade, Cross and Earsham. He turned to the Cross section and, after some thumbing, found an entry beginning: *Cross, Croyse, or Cruce.*

Bressingham was watching with jiffling impatience.

'Oh, never mind the early stuff, man!' he burst out. 'Skip all that stuff about Amazonian proud countesses, infangthef, waif and bread-and-ale.'

'Aha,' Ursula Bressingham said, handing coffee. 'It was you who wanted him to have the full flavour.'

'Oh, gosh, but there's reams of it,' Bressingham complained. 'Just a dip or two is enough to set the scene.'

Gently took his coffee and leafed on through heavy-pressed pages of irregular print. Strange, un-couth names caught his eye and words belonging to a forgotten language. He felt a curious helplessness, as though even where the language seemed plain he was not quite admitted to the *full* meaning. One was groping around in a nightmarish twilight peopled by half-monsters with half-human names. At last, this faded into a list of manors, church records, marbles, brasses, wills and charities, and then into untidy paragraphs and detached sentences about commons and streets and forgotten worthies.

'Am I missing something?'

'No – no!' Bressingham was reading now over his shoulder. 'You're nearly there. Don't miss a word. Keep reading from "Crofs is a neat compact town".'

Gently read. This was certainly more interesting.

Here Armstrong was mainly recording impressions. He gave a sharp impression of the Cross of his day, where the contaminated 'Meer' 'stank exceedingly'. Dirtftreet was 'properly enough fo called' but the ftreets about the market were newly paved, and summing up he concluded that Cross was 'one of the moft agreeable towns we have seen'. And that was Cross, Croyse or Cruce, apart from two biographical stop-presses. One was short and dealt with a John Spilwan. The other was longer. And it was a bomb.

'In this parifh,' Gently read, 'lived one Mr Harrifon, who was a curious collector of gold coins, from Pompey the Great to Honorius and Arcadius, and more modern times, up to VIIIth Henry; to which fome myftery is attached, they not being found in the houfe at his death. He was a very curious perfon, and lived in the houfe in which Robert Kent, fen., fince dwelt, which was adorned in a very odd manner: in the parlour ftood the effigy of a man, which had a speaking trumpet, put through the wall into the yard, fixed to his mouth, fo that upon one's entering the room it ufed to bid him welcome, by a fervant's fpeaking into the trumpet in the yard.

'On the parlour door you may read the following diftich in brafs capitals, in-laid in the wood:

'RECTA, PATENS, FELIX, JESUS, VIA,
    JANUA, VITA,
'ALPHA, DOCET, VERBUM, DUCIT,
    OMEGA, BEAT.

'And on the ftair-cafe door is a brafs plate, with a circle engraved thereon, equally divided by the twenty-four letters, and this diftich, in capitals of lead, in-laid in the wood:

   'DIFFICILIS, CELS – FERA, PORTA, OLYMPI,
   'FIT, FACILIS, FIDEI, CARDINE, CLAVE, MANU.'

Behind Gently, Bressingham gave a little gasp, as though he still couldn't quite believe what he was reading. Gently silently read the passage twice, then laid the book open on the table.

'So that's what we're dealing with!'

Bressingham nodded, puppet-like. 'Oh Lord! Doesn't it feel like meeting a ghost?'

'You're right . . . it's fantastic.'

'It just doesn't happen. Yet there it is . . . tucked away in Armstrong.'

Yes, there it was – and already a little legendary when Armstrong was writing in 1781. From the way it read Bressingham had probably been right when he'd placed his man in the seventeenth century. And subsequently the house had fallen into the hands of people who knew nothing of the significance of the door and its Latin, and then all that remained was the name and the fable – and an anecdote in Armstrong, which had lost its connection. Until . . .

'Do you think old Peachment had wit enough?'

'Gosh, yes. He had all his marbles.'

'He was deaf,' Ursula Bressingham put in. 'That's why people thought he was a little peculiar. But he was sharp. My father was a horse-dealer and he did business with Peachey in the old days. Peachey and Dadda used to play chess. I can remember him coming to the van.'

'But even if he identified the house, that's still a long way from finding the coins.'

'Oh dear, oh dear!' Bressingham exclaimed. 'What does it matter? We know he *did* find them.'

'Do we?'

'Yes – it has to be! There's that scrap of blue paper, remember? Oh my goodness, it was the very same paper that Harrison wrapped the angel in himself!'

Gently shook his head. 'Peachment wouldn't have been the first searcher. Harrison's heirs would have ransacked the house. Then there was this fellow – Robert Kent, senior – and the people who had the place when Armstrong knew it. Do you think they didn't search?'

'But they didn't find!' Bressingham jigged up and down with impatience. 'Look – they didn't know the first thing about it – that Harrison kept the collection in the storeroom.'

'You mean the orgy-room?'

'Oh, foof!' Bressingham waggled his plump shoulders. That was before I read this – it wasn't a bad guess, on the evidence. But now – look – it falls into place. Didn't we reckon it might be a strong-room? And Armstrong's brass plate is the final proof – because it's missing, we know what it was.'

Gently grinned. 'Yes – a double security.'

'You guessed that did you?' Bressingham sounded disappointed.

'If there's a bolt inside with no obvious purpose, you naturally look for a way to work it from outside.'

'Yes . . . well!' Bressingham waved his hands. 'The point is that Armstrong didn't know this. When the plate was in position it simply looked like decoration, all of a piece with the moulding and the Latin. And not knowing that, he didn't know what the room was, and ten to one nobody else did either. So they'd go pulling up the floors and ripping out wainscot, and never give the old linen-closet a thought.'

'But Peachment did know?'

'Isn't it obvious?'

Gently shrugged. 'Not so obvious as one thing! You and I both went over that room and found nothing suggestive, nor signs of interference.'

'So we don't know the secret!'

'If there's a secret.'

'Oh, my dear man!' Bressingham wrung his hands. 'It simply *has* to be there. It's in the logic of the house. It's because it's so tricky that the others didn't find it.'

Gently shook his head. It was academic anyway – the cache would be empty even if they found it. That fabulous collection, from Pompey to VIIIth Henry, had taken wing and flown from its ancient home. But was Peachment, beyond doubt, its liberator, or had it livanted at much earlier date – perhaps spirited away by some knee-breeched servant, before its eccentric collector was cold? Much more likely! The servants would know of it, would probably have watched Harrison manipulate the door. Then, when he died, a clean sweep, and some linen shoved on the shelves to confuse inquiry . . . the bolt on the door had never been forced, as it must have been if Harrison had died with its secret.

'It comes back to this – a medal and a coin – your bit of blue paper notwithstanding. That's all we're certain about just now . . . apart from some doubtful evidence I know of. No doubt they were part of this old collection, and that accounts for their fine condition. But it doesn't follow that Peachment found it, or that it was ever there for him to find.'

'Oh, you terrible man!' Bressingham groaned. 'No, you'd never make a dealer.'

'I've been spoiled,' Gently grinned. 'Too much homicide. It makes you an addict of hard fact.'

'But the paper is a fact!'

'Perhaps. Only you didn't actually examine the paper. It could have been a scrap from a sugar-bag, or the wrapper from a package of matches. But even if it was what you think it was, it doesn't prove that Peachment found the collection. Paper and all, the coin could have been lost, then found by Peachment in his poking around.'

'And the medal too?'

'Why not? Perhaps one rotting floorboard hid them both.'

'I despair of this man,' Bressingham said to his wife. 'He doesn't have a soul. What could you sell him?'

Ursula Bressingham shrugged very slightly, her intense eyes watching Gently.

'I think he is wrong,' she said. 'There is gold. And I think the Superintendent knows it.'

'Then he's an old fox,' Bressingham said.

'He doesn't want to believe in it,' Ursula Bressingham said. 'It's against himself he is arguing. But there is gold. And he knows it.'

She wasn't smiling; in fact, you got the impression she never smiled. Just with her eyes, sometimes. She had the features of a queen.

CHAPTER ELEVEN

T HEY WENT OVER the text again, Bressingham
leaning on the table beside Gently. The effigy
with the speaking-tube, Bressingham was positive, had
some connection with the priest-hole. He mourned
the loss of the parlour door, which had been tastelessly
replaced in the nineteenth century, and tortured
himself with the notion of the deeds being sent for
pulping by the Diocesan Registry. Then he listed the
coins: Pompey, Honorius, Arcadius and VIIIth Henry.
A double-rose crown of the latter, he opined, would
fetch over a hundred in EF. A Milanese *solidus* of
Honorius would be worth around sixty, but the earlier
Romans came higher – the Pompey might run to half
a thou.

'Just imagine a cabinet full of the stuff.' His eyes
went dreamy over the idea. 'What a sale it would be
. . . how the devils would flock there! A million
quidsworth . . . could be more.'

'A million quidsworth?'

'Yes. Easily. The goods were around in Harrison's

day. I'll bet the old boy had filled all the gaps – unique pieces, oh, my gosh!'

A sort of flat box thing full of coins . . . dully gleaming in the light of the hurricane. The kids had seen it . . . and who else? A million quid. And no bolt on the door.

'How would they get rid of it, if they pinched it?'

Bressingham's pale eyebrows hooked up in anguish. 'Don't talk about that. It makes me shudder. If they didn't know the value, the morons might melt it.'

'But if they did know the value?'

'They'd still need a connection. Unless they were specialists, I think they'd be stuck. My gosh, you've got to find it before the swine get desperate. It's around, I know it is. For heaven's sake don't write it off.'

'We're searching.'

Bressingham stared at him. 'Please believe in it,' he said. 'Somehow I feel responsible. As though old Harrison were at my shoulder.'

There was small point in fetching out the Sceptre, which in any case was snowbound in the George's yard. Gently set off on foot for the warehouse, a freshly lit pipe in his mouth.

They'd cleared Water Street, and a fussy bulldozer was shunting snow by the car-park. The wind had dropped. Above, the sky was glooming dull, but looked empty. A skein of geese was passing over, probably heading for the nearest estuary: twelve, with wings slow-going. Gently could just catch the 'woo' of their pinions.

On the sale-ground yesterday's slide was buried deep

under new falls, but a plentiful scatter of prints showed where Dinno and his pals had passed. The bulldozer, no doubt at Gissing's instance, had made a run down one side of Frenze Street, throwing up a flange of packed snow that overtopped the hedge at Harrisons. Wheel-tracks showed on the ploughed surface. The Wolseley was parked outside the warehouse. The bulldozer had also been in the yard, but towards the house stretched unmarked snow. Gently crossed to the warehouse and went in.

'Hullo . . . how is it going?'

Gissing showed at the office door. He looked dazed, and was vaguely wiping his hands on his coat.

'We've found some tyres hidden away . . . there's no doubt that Colkett was on the game.'

'We knew that last night.'

'But all the same . . .' He shrugged, and got out a cigarette.

Scoles and two other men were distantly ferreting among stacks of cases and dust-sheeted furniture. The warehouse was nominally lighted by half a dozen bulbs strung down the centre. It was cold as an ice-store, oddly churchlike, and smelt of paraffin and old news-print. A depressing place. Just walking in there seemed to throw a shadow on life.

A bit of theft, in a place like that, was probably needed to cheer a man up . . .

'I've been on the phone . . . there's nothing certain.'

Gissing backed off into the office. Gently followed. Colkett's stove was going. The office itself had a turned-over look.

'They've got a road clear, but now it's the trains. They reckon to have them running by teatime. Norchester rang. They've heard of a bloke who was trying for a lift at a transport café.'

'A bloke like ours?'

Gissing nodded blankly. 'Looking for transport going towards London.'

'Which is this way.'

'Yes – but he needn't have got off here.'

Gently pondered. It was scarcely likely that Colkett had skipped to London. He wouldn't have got there in any case, the roads being how they were. It was still odds on, if he'd got his lift, that he'd been stuck between Cross and Norchester – which being so, with a road now clear, he'd be arriving home at any moment.

'You still have a man outside Hallet's?'

'Yes.' Gissing rested his bottom on the table. 'Only . . . well, I've checked on all the stranded vehicles. There's no sign that he spent the night on the road.'

'So what's your theory?'

Gissing shook his head. He hadn't a theory – he just felt. Somehow, somewhere, the iniquitous Colkett was slipping past the well-laid snares of inquiry.

Scoles came in.

'Sir, we've found some batteries . . .'

Gissing hoisted his butt-end from the table and went. The warehouse faintly echoed his dragging footsteps, alongside the brisker footing of Scoles.

Gently stayed with them. There was something compulsive about the utter dreariness of the warehouse. The longer you remained there, the more you felt a reluctant sympathy for Colkett. Day in, day out, winter and summer, he maintained his lonely watch there, broken only occasionally by the routine of checking a load in or out. And some days would lack even that diversion. Then, he was solitary for nine hours – trying to kill the time with sporting papers, and moody wanderings round the soulless building. The kids cheeked him: he probably encouraged it. He would dearly have loved to make friends with old Peachment. A mug of tea would always be waiting for any casual he could pick up a chat with.

And his stealing – was it really genuine, or just a defence against grinding boredom? All over the warehouse they were turning up his pitiful, magpie hoards. Nothing valuable. A box of batteries, a pair of cycle tyres, a set of wheel-trims. Perhaps he'd never even tried to flog it, wouldn't know how. Just an escape . . .

Glumly, Gently went over the office, where the weary Gissing had searched before him. It was all of a piece. Everywhere tokens of boredom without resource. Girlie mags, a thumbed *Kama Sutra*, football papers with marked forecasts. Nude pin-ups, with air-brushed vacancies heavily restored in black pencil. In the waste-bin he found a screw of blue paper which he eagerly unfolded. No luck. It contained salt, was obviously a discard from a packet of crisps.

He wandered out into the warehouse, much as Colkett would have wandered out. It was probably the smell more than anything that made your heart sink out there. Not a strong smell, but sweetish, like a pile of old boots: sleazy, decaying. The smell of worn-out, forgotten things . . .

'When do you think you'll be through?'

At his interruption, they all stopped. They'd been manhandling forty heavy steel cabinets stood, perversely, with doors facing doors. Along with Scoles was D.C. Abbotts and a ginger-haired man, Brewer, Gissing's sergeant. The latter hadn't been introduced to Gently; he stood stiffly, almost at attention.

'I don't know . . . we're still finding things. We can't afford a slip-up.'

But some of the buck had gone out of Gissing – you felt he'd look twice at a good excuse.

'You've got enough to do Colkett.'

'Yes. But we have to be thorough.'

'You could finish this job at your leisure.'

Gissing wavered, then said, 'There's also the other thing . . .'

The other thing! Was he still hoping to strike gold in one of those hoards? Working back now into deserts of furniture, which clearly had filled the deep recesses for years?

'That's probably pre-Colkett country, back there.'

Gissing frowned, too tired to pick it up quickly.

'I don't know . . .'

He turned away from Gently: a gesture. He wasn't done yet.

And somehow, his obstinacy was infectious, like the blind belief of a religious fanatic. Wouldn't a faith so strong find its object – or perhaps create one, if none existed?

Gently watched a while, then returned to the office. He was just in time to catch the phone. It came from the desk: a routine call. Still, there wasn't any sign of Colkett.

He rang the desk when he went to lunch, then again after lunch. He came away frowning. Now, it was twenty-four hours since anyone had set eyes on Colkett. Had the stupid fellow really skipped, some-how sensing the net was laid for him – or was he in some other trouble, out there in the snows?

Gently took his coffee into the lounge and smoked a pipe over the problem. If Colkett had skipped, it was because he was deeper in the business than Gently was allowing. Yet that was difficult to swallow. Gently was sure he'd read Colkett's character right. A furtive rogue, but not a true villain, and not a man to resort to violence. Also, if the collection of coins were involved, stealing them was outside Colkett's scope. He wouldn't dare: it was that simple. To pocket one would be the strength of him. How, then . . . ?

Gently smoked and drank. If the collection of coins were involved . . . A million pounds' worth of antique gold, almost begging to be walked off with. Spread that information in town and there'd be a traffic jam up the A.12, and enough hot Jaguars parked in Frenze Street to start a Monte-Carlo Rally. Was that the way of it? Had Colkett passed his information to a high-powered outfit – who now, with the advent of Gently, had decided to vanish Colkett for a while? Gently pon-dered, then shook his head. Even for this Colkett wasn't man enough! What did he know of high-powered outfits, or of how to profit by tipping them off?

Could he have been involved accidentally? That would square better with Colkett's character – was, in fact, the supposition which Gently had been favouring all along. Colkett, hearing about the coins, would doubtless be eager to see them for himself, and going along there at the critical time, might well have been witness to the crime. But this presupposed that the criminals had been tipped off from some other quarter, which was even more improbable than Colkett tipping them off himself. Young Peachment? Hardly! He'd nothing to gain: if he knew of the coins he'd keep it dark. And a casual observer from Thingoe Road was as unlikely as Colkett to have connections. The kids? No . . . the more you looked at it, the less credible did it seem.

Then Gently hesitated. Because . . . yes, there was one way that tip could have gone. He bit on his pipe scowlingly, trying to dispose of the treacherous thought. But it had to be dealt with. Slowly, unwill-ingly, he began checking off the score . . . Phil Bressingham was one of the kids: and Phil could have told his father.

The answer?

He sat a long while, the coffee gone cold in the cup beside him. It fitted, he knew it fitted – all the way down the line. If Bressingham were bent, he could have used that information. Bressingham had his connections in town. He was in the trade, he knew the channels. Worse, he was in town on the day of the crime. That was his alibi, oh yes! – but it could be his downfall too. It gave him opportunity to pass on his tip, to set up the job for when he was absent . . .

Gently got up and strode down to the windows, stood gazing out at the snowbound Mere. Bressingham was a dealer, a professional sprucer . . . not beyond him to put on such an act. And hadn't he given a little flick at Colkett, after seeing where Gently's suspicions were tending – perhaps then to report to his associates in town, with the suggestion that Colkett be taken care of?

No – it was too ugly! He kicked at the carpet. It fell together, but he couldn't believe it. Good Lord, if he'd given Colkett the benefit of exclusion-by-character, couldn't he do the same for Bressingham? And again, what interest could Bressingham have, if guilty, in drawing Gently's attention to the existence of the collection? The notion was mad! It'd be all the other way – he'd pooh-pooh everything to do with the coins.

So you were left again with the improbability of a gang crime, and doubts about whether the collection did exist. And nothing to indicate Colkett's where-abouts, or why he had suddenly decided to go missing. Gently scowled some more at the Mere. However you looked at it, Colkett was a witness. And if Colkett wasn't going to come to them, then it was time some-body went after Colkett.

He got his coat again and went out to the courtyard. The snow had been shovelled against the walls in heaps. With a lot of wheel-slip he extricated the Sceptre, and nursed it cautiously into the street.

It was irrational: he knew that. He didn't have a hope of finding Colkett. It wasn't even fair to say he had a hunch, or the ghost of a lead that might have paid off. What he was feeling now was a vague irritation, a sense of having failed somewhere. Failed who? When you came down to it . . . perhaps a feeling he'd failed Colkett. Ridiculous? Yes: but he couldn't get rid of it. Perhaps just Gently's presence had been Colkett's undoing. And Gently should have seen that, should have sensed the pattern, played his cards a little differently. Instead, he'd been bearing down on Colkett, making it evident he thought him important. And now, like Bressingham, he was feeling responsible. He'd got Colkett into this – he must get him out!

The expedition nearly ended a hundred yards from the town limits. Only a single track had been ploughed along the twisty link with the A.140. Backing to let a mail-van by, Gently dropped a rear wheel into a gully: it wasn't deep, but it was enough. Fortunately, the postmen were there to shove him. He drove on swearing, his rear-end skewing at the slightest pressure on the gas. The road had been salted, but because of the low temperature the salt was failing to take effect.

At Broome he sought the local constable, a heavy-bodied countryman named Money. Money gratefully sat in the Sceptre for a spell and smoked the cigarette Gently offered him.

'Would you know Colkett by sight?'

159

'No, sir, but they gave me a very plain description.'

'When did the traffic stop coming through yester-day?'

'Reckon about six, sir. There wasn't much after that.'

'When did you start watching for a bus?'

'Well, sir' – Money took a long puff – 'there was one due in here at half seven. I didn't come out very long before that.'

'So you weren't actually watching for Colkett?'

'Well . . . no, sir. That wasn't the message. I'd to meet the bus, but it never turned up—'

'That's all right,' Gently shrugged. 'As long as we know.'

Thus in effect there'd been no watch for Colkett: the net was wide open at the Cross end. He could have dropped off a truck or gone sailing through, and nobody have been any the wiser.

'Were any vehicles stuck in the village last night?'

'Two, sir. But they came from the other direction.'

'How are the buses now?'

'There's the main-road service. They're dropping passengers here for Cross.'

Gently drove on. The main road was packed snow, stained and crumbling, running between piles made by the ploughs and between steep, wind-sculptured drifts. Beyond were snow-deep fields with their hedges drifted under, and black field-oaks with frosted beards, standing dwarfish in the blank whiteness. He passed numerous abandoned cars. The road-teams had shunted them on to the verges. A truck, lettered

Eastwich Tar and Gravel Co., had left the road and canted into a drift. You got the impression that something frightening had happened out here on the road, in the dark night: more than just a blizzard of snow. As though the Valkyries had ridden by.

And Colkett, caught up in this lot? Perhaps left in the middle, thumbing a lift? Maybe they wouldn't see Colkett again till the bruised earth showed through the rotting snow.

He reached Tattishall Crossroads and turned down to the village. At the Police House he found the constable's wife. She'd helped to organize arrangements at the school, but she could only confirm her husband's report.

'Here's the list of names and addresses – only two of them came from Cross. They were mostly girls who work in Norchester. We had to let their parents know.'

Both of the Cross passengers had been girls. Gently noted their names and addresses. The constable's wife, an efficient young lady, quickly brewed him a cup of tea.

'It was pretty bad out this way last night?'

The constable's wife sucked breath through her teeth. It had been the devil: she'd almost got lost just going down to the school from the Police House.

'It was the snow and the wind together . . . and the cold. It sort of confused you. Some of the girls looked knocked out. I don't think they'd have stuck a night in the bus.'

'Better that than out in the open.'

'They'd have been dead,' she said decidedly.

He left her warm kitchen reluctantly and slithered the Sceptre back to the A.140. About a hundred yards past the crossroads he noticed a crater, from which doubtless the stranded bus had been dug. A desolate spot! No stitch of shelter: just the wide sweep of the fields.

Thirty minutes later he was coasting into Norchester over loose sanded snow, like brown sugar. The Wagon Wheel, the roadhouse where Colkett had been seen, was on the outskirts, near the ring-road. Gently parked and went in. He was met by soft music. Two girls were lounging at a brightly lit counter; behind them, through a hatch that opened over a hotplate, he could see a man in white overalls, frying eggs. He beckoned one of the girls.

'Police . . . I'm inquiring about the man who was seen here yesterday.'

The girl gazed starrily for a moment, then put her head through the hatch.

'Lew!'

Lew came. It was he who'd noticed Colkett, while he'd been serving during the girls' lunch-break. A short, thick-faced man, he kept wiping his hands as he went over his story with Gently. Yes, the bloke answered to Gently's description of him. He'd come in there about half-past two. He'd ordered a meal and paid with a fiver (this was an unexpected bonus!). Then he'd sat eating and reading a paper until a couple of truckers came in, when he'd struck up a conversation and asked them if they were heading for London.

'Do you know the drivers?'

'Not their names. I've seen them in here a few times before.'

'Do you know who they drive for?'

Lew shook his head. 'But I reckon they're local, the way they speak.'

The starry-eyed girl giggled. 'The fair one's local. I've seen him dancing up at the Samson.'

His name was Fred, and he was a bit cheeky – but that was the limit of her information.

'Do you know if our man got a lift?'

'No . . . I didn't pay much attention,' Lew said. 'When did the drivers leave?'

'I think they hung on a bit, waiting to see if the snow would ease.'

He put more questions, but that was the gist of it, and perhaps he was lucky to get so much. Yesterday afternoon there'd been plenty of drivers hanging about there like Fred and his mate. Then, some time after four, the snow had cleared for a spell, and a few of the bold ones had started out . . . along with them Colkett, beyond doubt: into the snow, vaguely Londonwards.

And that was all: he'd known as much when he'd skewed the Sceptre out of the George's yard. Only now he'd seen what the snow had been like, could make a sombre guess or two.

He left Lew with instructions to watch out for Fred and to ask him to contact the City Police; then he pointed the Sceptre south again and began his gloomy return to Cross.

★ ★ ★

163

It was dark when he arrived. He drove direct to the Police Station. Outside, he noticed Gissing's Wolseley with misted windows, recently parked.

'The Inspector's just come in, sir,' the desk sergeant told him. 'He asked me to try to contact you.'

'What's new?'

'I think he's found something, sir. He was carrying a package wrapped with newspaper.'

Gently hastened to the office, knocked, went in. He found Gissing and his team grouped round the desk. On the desk was an opened-out sheet of newspaper with a green object lying on it. As Gently approached, Gissing looked up at him – the face of a weary martyr triumphant.

'Reckon this time we *have* nailed him, sir,' he said huskily.

The object on the paper was a bloodstained cosh.

CHAPTER TWELVE

IT WAS A crude, childish weapon, made from a length of plastic hose, weighted at one end with a carriage-bolt and whipped with common brown string. It was dirty, and the string was scuffed, suggesting it had been carried in someone's pocket. The smears on the weighted end were brown, but Gently had no doubt they were blood.

'Where did you find it?'

'Right at the back. Behind that stack of old furniture.'

In the very place, in fact, which Gently had suggested they needn't search.

'How long had it been there?'

'Not very long. It was lying in some fluff, but it wasn't dusty. He'll have chucked it over there to get rid of it . . . he couldn't know we'd shift all that furniture.'

No – he couldn't! Gently shrugged a little guiltily. That cosh might have lain there till Kingdom-come. It had taken the massive faith of a Gissing to sift the warehouse to its ultimate fluff.

'Looks like he carted it around with him, sir . . . had it for quite a while, I reckon. Never quite got round to using it. Not until old Peachment caught him.'

'Is that how you read it?'

'Well – yes, sir.' Gissing gave him the blank look. 'This is the weapon, I'd say that's certain. It'd account for all that bruising.'

'And Colkett carried it?'

'Must have done, sir. That cosh has been in someone's pocket.'

'He didn't strike me as that sort.'

Gissing shook his head – you lived and learned about chummies!

Gently picked up the cosh – there would be no dabs on the ribbed surface of the hose – and twisted it slowly between his fingers, noting details of its fashioning. Crude: that must be the word. The product of skill-less, impatient fingers. The whipping put on awry and knotted, the hose sawn off with an inept knife. Colkett's work? Not characteristic: he, with so much time on his hands. He'd have neatly severed that hose with a hacksaw and whipped it correctly, perhaps with marlin.

Yet this was the weapon . . . found where it was found. Who but Colkett could have tossed it there?

He laid the cosh down.

'Better get it to your lab.'

'Yes, sir. And step up the hunt for Colkett.'

Gently nodded. It was a murder-hunt now. No longer a matter of bobbies meeting buses.

'I reckon he did skip, sir,' Gissing said musingly. 'He

166

must have guessed we were getting close to him. He never intended to come back here . . . he just cashed the coin, and hopped it.'

'But why go to Norchester to do that?'

'Why?' Gissing stared. 'It's where he would go.'

'Even though he were planning to skip to London?'

'Well . . .' Gissing took refuge in blankness.

'Perhaps he hadn't made his mind up, sir,' Scoles suggested. 'He was just raising the cash, ready for a flit. Then maybe he realized we'd hear about the coin, so he decided to keep moving.'

'He could realize that without going to Norchester.'

'I don't know, sir. He isn't very bright.'

'Then how did he come to realize it at all?'

Scoles coloured and shut up.

The point was that none of this was fitting Colkett! Gently stared from one to another of the little group. They were seeing it too simply, too narrowly, determined to abide by the main fact . . .

'Look – let's face up to what we're implying! We're saying that Colkett is a sadist and a killer – that he carried a cosh, and that when old Peachment caught him he beat Peachment up before he killed him. And all we know to date about Colkett is that he's a rogue with no record of violence – and a local fellow. Not a man, you'd think, who'd run off to hide in London. But that's what we're saying, and what we'll have to make good to the Director of Public Prosecutions.'

Gissing shifted uneasily. 'But that's how it is.'

'You're happy to go along with that?'

'Now we've found the cosh—'

'You haven't tied it to him. He may have picked it up when they found the body.'

Gissing shook his head, looking round at the others. They were staring silently, indignant almost.

'I don't know . . . yes, we'll go along with it. I reckon we've got our case now . . .'

Gently shrugged. At least, he'd tried! And all that really mattered was catching Colkett . . . He gave them an account of his visit to Norchester, and the details of the truck-driver he'd got at the Wagon Wheel. Gissing seemed cheered.

'I'll get on to Norchester . . . perhaps they can trace him right away. Do you reckon chummie made it to London?'

Gently shrugged again, meaning nothing.

It was the next morning when Norchester CID interviewed a blond truck-driver named Frederick Hall, who had picked up a passenger at the Wagon Wheel on the afternoon of the big snow-up. The description of the passenger fitted Colkett. He'd asked Hall if he were going towards London. Hall told him he was turning off at Beeston Corner, and the man replied that it would do. Hall had set out at half-past four, and reached Beeston Corner about five-fifteen. It was snowing heavily, and Hall offered to take the man on with him to his destination at Elmham Market. The man, however, refused, saying he wanted to be getting on, and the last Hall saw of him was walking down the road in the London direction.

Gissing showed the message to Gently.

'Not much doubt now where he was heading.'

But a good deal of doubt about whether he'd got there, at such a time, on such a night.

'Let's look at a map.'

Gissing produced a one-inch ordnance map from his desk. Beeston Corner was only a mile up the A.140 from Broome.

'It would do – that's what he said.'

'Well . . . it was getting him on towards London.'

Gently tapped the map. 'At Beeston Corner he was exactly two miles from home! If he were heading there, it would do – but scarcely if he were heading for London. In that case he'd have hung on at the road-house, looking for transport going straight through.'

'You mean . . . he came this way?' Gissing stared.

'Isn't that what the message is saying? Hall "last saw him walking down the road". You can bet he wasn't walking to London.'

'But he didn't turn up here!'

'Do we know that?'

'We—' Gissing broke off, his look woeful.

'All we know is he didn't come home – or if he did, he spotted your watchdog.'

'But then, where would he have gone?'

'One place we know of.'

Gissing started. 'Not the warehouse!'

'Why not? He had the key, and he needed to get a night's shelter somewhere.'

Gissing got up agitatedly from his chair and went to stare out of the window. He didn't want to believe that! It was upsetting all his preconceptions. If Colkett had come lamb-like home it was giving a knock to the image of guilt: Gissing wanted Colkett skulking about the London back-streets – where, in fact, the Metropolitan Police were now watching for him.

'Did you notice any traces at the warehouse yesterday?'

'No.'

'Wait a moment! Give it some thought.'

Gissing came back unhappily from the window and sat down lumpishly in his chair.

'I wasn't noticing—'

'Think – when you got there. Did you see any tracks leading from the warehouse?'

Gissing miserably tried to get a picture in focus, but had to end up shaking his head.

'I don't know . . . I was tired. Perhaps one of the others can remember. You see, I was only thinking . . . I believe there was snow drifted against the door.'

'Let's go inside.'

Gissing frowned, tried.

'Was the door of the office open or closed?'

'Closed . . . locked.'

'When you unlocked the door, did the office seem warmer than the warehouse outside?'

But he didn't know, couldn't be sure. Gissing had gone there for one purpose only. Flogging his tired body, he'd achieved that purpose; the rest was just a great blankness.

'But if he came back . . . where is he now?'

The sixty-four-dollar question! He might even have

resumed his broken journey, and be now indeed roaming London. Yet . . . Colkett?

'I think he's here. Probably hiding with some acquaintance.'

Gissing grabbed at it. 'Yes – that's possible! We'd better start making inquiries.'

Gently hesitated. 'Surely – even Colkett! – has got a woman in his background, somewhere?'

'A woman . . .'

Gissing toyed with the notion as though it were a wonderful, a novel idea.

And perhaps it was. Gently left the Police Station wondering if he hadn't dropped a penny by accident. Suddenly he was seeing the photographs of those bruises – so many, so widespread, and yet so moderate. The deed of a woman, a woman with a cosh? Old Peachment plainly had not defended himself: he'd stood there taking it, blow after blow, till the last one sent him crashing down the stairs. A woman he knew and hadn't feared, and yet who'd been armed and had sadistically beaten him. Who'd made that cosh, who knew Colkett . . . who might be hiding Colkett now.

Only one snag – no obvious suspect! They knew of no woman who associated with Colkett; and judging from his knowledge of the man, Gently had to admit the hypothesis improbable. Colkett was a loner, fearful at the bottom of him; he'd shrink from associates of either sex. His commerce with women would be furtive and transient – likely, he'd never slept with one in his life.

Yet was that necessary?

Couldn't the woman here predicated be dominating Colkett by sheer strength of character?

After all, right under their noses, was *one* woman with whom he was in daily contact . . .

Gently turned aside into Playford Road, where snow lay piled on the pavements in grimy heaps. Hallet's was open, and in the doorway opposite Metcalfe's relief stood easing his feet. Gently nodded to him: he saluted. Behind her vegetables, Mrs Hallet watched gnome-like. Gently drifted across to the shop. She rose slowly, keeping her hands in her pockets.

'Got him yet?'

Gently shook his head. Mrs Hallet stared at him with hard eyes.

'Taking your time about it, aren't you? Where do you reckon he's got to, then?'

Gently shrugged. 'Perhaps you can tell us.'

'Me!' Immediately, the hard eyes sparked with aggression.

'You know him as well as anyone, don't you?'

'Huh!' She made a gesture with her head.

'Well . . . doesn't he meal with you?'

'Breakfast and tea. Doesn't mean to say I know his business.'

'And the evenings, sometimes?'

'Not Cokey. Always off to the boozer, he is.'

'But – sometimes?'

She stared at him spitefully. 'I'm telling you – I don't know his business! Just the bleeding lodger, that's what he is, and I don't have any other truck with him.'

'He doesn't bring his friends here?'

'He ain't got none.'

'A woman?'

'Huh – that's a laugh! Screwing himself with a dirty book is all he knows about women.'

There was a bitterness in the way she said it, as though Colkett might have been a disappointment. A comic scene of frustrated seduction suddenly suggested itself to Gently.

'Like that, was he?'

'Yeah – like that. So you can forget about his women.'

Gently nodded.

Mrs Hallet sniffed. 'He'd run a bleeding mile,' she said.

Gently tramped away up Playford Road, kicking at occasional nuggets of snow. Not Mrs Hallet – but still, there might be a woman who fitted somewhere. A woman, probably, of small sex, who'd never made a pass at Colkett – not homosexual, but frigid . . . the presence of sex without its demand.

From Thingoe Road? The finger pointed there, if the woman were known to old Peachment. And to Thingoe Road, not to the warehouse, might Colkett have gone on that snowy night . . .

Pondering, he took his way to Frenze Street, back to the cockpit of the curious business. The front of Harrisons looked dirty and dead against the snow and the dull sky. Yesterday's tracks were still hard-frozen, showing where Gissing and his men had gone: he'd been right about the snow drift against the warehouse:

you could see where the opening door had swept up a pile. Around Harrisons the snow remained unprinted, sealing the old house in its shabbiness. Gently climbed a packing-case to look over the wall. Solid drifts, reaching the lower windows.

He heard a whoop behind him, and climbed down. Dinno and his mates had charged out of the passage. Catching sight of Gently, they galloped swervingly away from him, then pulled up short, looking foolish. Gently walked over to them. This was a larger group than those he'd talked to before. In particular, he noticed a round-cheeked youngster who flushed rosily when he felt Gently's eye on him.

'Hullo . . . Phillip Bressingham?'

The boy simply blushed. Dinno, with Moosh backing him, strutted forward to take command.

'Course he's Pills, mister . . . you going to pinch him?'

They giggled nervously, eyes rolling at Gently. Phillip Bressingham drooped his head, tried to shrink away among the others.

Dinno's hands crept compulsively into his pockets. 'You still looking for old Cokey, mister?' he said. 'We haven't seen him round here no more. Reckon old Cokey's gone away.'

'You reckon that, do you?' Gently said.

'He's gone away,' Dinno repeated firmly. 'He got the gold, didn't he, mister? We shan't see old Cokey no more.'

He stared intently at Gently, challenging him. Moosh, just behind, had a glassy stare. The rest watched breathlessly, eyes helpless, catching at the words in a sort of stupor.

'I think you're kidding me,' Gently smiled. 'I don't think there ever was any gold.'

'Cooh – no gold!' Dinno exclaimed, almost angrily. 'We saw it, didn't we? Didn't we see it?'

'Then where's it gone? Colkett didn't have it.'

'But he did, mister! We know he did.'

'How?'

Dinno's eyes flickered. 'Saw him.'

'Saw him?'

Dinno nodded. 'Time he came back here.'

There was a strange, tight, electric stillness, everyone there holding his breath. You could almost touch it.

Dinno's face looked pinched. His eyes were large, straining at Gently's. Gently's face had gone blank.

'When?' he said. 'When was this?'

'Mister, it's true—'

'Yes – but when?'

Dinno swallowed. 'Night before last.'

'The night before last!'

'It's true, mister! We see him here, didn't we Moosh?'

'Course we saw him,' Moosh said. 'He come out of the warehouse with a big old spanner.'

'A sort of wrench-thing,' Dinno said. 'He come out there an' locked the door. He was going over to the house to fetch the gold. Then he sees Moosh and me, and chases us.'

'What time was this?'

''Bout half-past seven. Moosh and me had been up the town.'

'Just you two?'

'Yes – we'd been up the town!'

'Tha's right, mister,' Moosh said. 'Up the town.'

Gently hunched his shoulders, staring at them. Was it a fact, or a bit of fantasy? The spanner detail sounded factual, but always that 'gold' struck a note of fable . . .

'Wasn't it snowing hard the night before last?'

'We don't care about snow,' Dinno said. 'Anyway, mister, it left off for a bit. That's why Moosh and me went out.'

'Where were you when you saw Colkett?'

'We was just coming through the gateway.'

'Running?'

'W . . . yes.'

'And Colkett didn't hear you?'

'W . . . no, he'd just come out. He was closing the door.'

'How did you know it was him?'

'You could see it was Cokey. There's that light in the passage, and he was flashing a torch.'

Gently nodded. 'Go on,' he said. 'Tell me what happened after that.'

'W . . . we hid up behind the gatepost, so we could see what old Cokey was up to. Then we see him go across the yard with this great old wrench-thing in his hand, an' Moosh, he coont keep quiet, he hailer: "Old Peachey's ghost'll come after you." Cooh, did he come for us! We didn't half run – he'd got that thing in his hand, too.'

'Did you come back again?'

'No we never. Reckon old Cokey would have murdered us.'

'He was suffn wild, he was,' Moosh said. 'Didn't like us watching him go for the gold.'

The 'gold' again! And that same odd tenseness – eyes, waiting to see how he'd take it. Did they know the difference between fact and fiction, or did the two merge, become real only in their effect? 'It's true, mister!' And if Gently accepted it, then it was real beyond fact . . .

'Right,' he said. 'Thanks for telling me. I'll have to think about this.'

'But we *did* see him, mister.'

'I'll believe you.'

They moved off slowly, as though dissatisfied.

Gently turned again to Harrisons, to the smooth witness of deep snow. But the snow, of course, was no longer a witness, if Colkett had been there the night before last. Plenty had fallen after half-past seven to cover the warehouseman's prints . . . and one remembered that, earlier the same day, he'd made a previous attempt to get in the house.

Gently crossed the snow with a few quick strides. Daylight was brightening the top end of the outhouse. The back door stood open – and lying on the ground near it were the wrenched-off padlock, hasp and staple.

He went in. Dinno's 'wrench-thing' stood against the wall, just inside. Along the passage, into the kitchen, were the wet traces of melted snow. They passed through the kitchen into the back corridor, and down the corridor to the stair. And there, where Peachment had lain, lay Colkett, his dead face grinning towards the kitchen.

His neck was broken. He was tumbled against the wall, and snow-water showed on the stairs above him. He had a wound on his forehead which had bled over his nose and his eyes were open, staring in horror. The knuckles of one hand were bruised and bloody and bruising showed on a protruding leg. The body was ice-cold, like frozen meat. Nevertheless, it had a faint smell of carrion.

Gently heard a sobbing gasp, and looked over his shoulder. Dinno had followed him into the house.

Dinno stood pale, huge-eyed, staring, drinking in the corpse in excited terror.

'Get out of here!' Gently bawled.

Dinno turned and ran without a word. Then, reaching the yard, he began shouting hysterically.

'Old Peachey's got Cokey ... old Peachey's got him!'

CHAPTER THIRTEEN

I T WAS A theory – and four hours later it was still the only theory. Gissing and his men got nothing from the house that Gently hadn't got in the first five minutes. Colkett had broken in: the snow-water showed he'd gone straight to the little storeroom: and there he'd been attacked by someone – or something – and hurled to his death down the stairs. Same bruising, same look of horror. In fact, a carbon-copy crime.

And like it or not, it gave you a shiver, set you thinking of the supernatural. Peachment, Colkett, both had gone to that room and met something frightful, and died in horror. Some mindless thing. It had stupefied them. They couldn't resist its demonic fury. And out, out of that room they had gone, flying down the stairs to their dooms . . .

Were such things possible? Had Harrison's spirit been chained to the room by his gold, a residual evil, that burst into violence when his secret hoard was threatened?

Well – Gently and Bressingham had searched the room without arousing a vengeful poltergeist – and as for the gold, if it had ever been there, it was gone by the time Colkett paid his visit. But perhaps it was the gold being removed that had wakened the ghost in the first place?

Nonsense, of course! And yet . . . That eery little shiver kept coming back.

One thing was certain: they could no longer keep this case off the front page. Dinno had seen to that. He'd sounded a tocsin through Cross. A crowd had begun to gather in Frenze Street almost before Gissing's men had got there, and Gissing had been obliged to call out more uniform men to clear the yard and seal-off the footway. And the crowd had remained there, freezing in the snow, watching the police comings and goings – their high-spot a glimpse of the shrouded stretcher on which the body was carried out to a van. Wemys, the stringer, was quickly there, and soon now would follow the vultures.

By two p.m. the police were through, and there was nothing left to watch at Harrisons. A Panda car remained to guard it, and a little sleet was dredging Frenze Street.

They held the conference in Gissing's office, with the i/c, Boyland, sitting in: Gently, Gissing, Sergeant Brewer, and the two D.C.s, Scoles and Abbotts. Gently personally had rung Sir Daynes, but Sir Daynes was still marooned at Merely. He'd fumed helplessly about the County Council, and besought Gently to play it cool with the Press. Well . . . if that were possible! Boyland brought with him a report from the lab. It confirmed that the blood on the cosh was of Peachment's group, and identified the hose as coming from Messrs Woolworths.

'At least it connects Colkett with Peachment's murder.'

Gissing seemed to draw nourishment from the thought. The door had slammed, but – alive or dead – Colkett was still Gissing's chummie.

'Do we have any lead at all?' Boyland asked. 'I mean, the fact is, there's a killer loose. When it comes to the crunch, I'm whipping-boy – I've got to know where I stand.'

Gissing shook his head. Boyland looked at Gently. Gently took some draws from his pipe.

'Just at the moment it's square one . . . Colkett was the man who knew the answers.'

'So what are we doing?' Boyland sounded plaintive.

'We're beginning again,' Gently shrugged. 'The old routine. Checking round Colkett. Watching for the loot to turn up.'

'But isn't there . . . anyone?'

Gently hesitated. 'We'll be checking the movements of a few people. The Hallets, young Peachment, perhaps some others. Plus a lot of leg-work in Thingoe Road.'

'What about dabs?'

'We don't seem to be lucky.'

'There's only a few smears,' Brewer said. 'We did get some good ones, but they're Mr Bressingham's. The Super told us we'd find them there.'

'And that's all?'

'That's all, sir. Except the water on the floor.'

'It's bloody witchcraft,' Boyland said. He pulled out a sudden, fat sigh.

Colkett hadn't been robbed. Lying on the desk were the pathetic gleanings from his pockets: coins, cigarettes, an old lighter, a comb, keys, and a wallet containing, *inter alia*, eight fivers. Either the murderer had been in too much of a hurry or else he didn't stoop to such small game . . . or was there another angle? Had he tried deliberately to give an impression of something uncanny?

Gently stuffed his pipe away.

'Right – let's try to make sense of it,' he said. 'Colkett was killed for some clear-cut motive. Peachment's death may have been unpremeditated, but Colkett's wasn't. So why did he die?'

Gissing stared heavily. 'Because he knew too much?'

Gently nodded. 'A fair suggestion! He was in a position to watch Harrisons, to witness whatever was going on there. And he did witness something – Peachment's killing – perhaps saw it through the window, from the perch by the wall. The youngsters had kidded him about Peachment's gold, and the next night he went to see it for himself. So he saw the murder and – this is the point – he tried to cover up for the murderer. The murderer left his cosh on the scene, and Colkett found it and got rid of it. Motive?'

They gazed at him.

'Blackmail,' Brewer said.

Gently shook his head. 'I don't think so. Simply, I

182

can't see Colkett as a blackmailer – and I think he'd have died the sooner if he'd tried it.'

'Perhaps the murderer was a friend, sir,' Scoles said.

'Perhaps,' Gently said. 'It makes more sense. But we'll leave that point for the moment and see what happened after Peachment's death. The body is found – the weapon isn't found, neither is a piece of gold lying by the body. The bruises are odd, but you've no other reason for supposing Peachment's death wasn't an accident. So the inquest goes off quietly, and for a month nothing happens. Then, surprisingly, I come on the scene, suggesting the police aren't happy after all. Worse still, I begin leaning on Colkett, and you begin double-checking his movements – and Colkett is vulnerable: he's already lied to you about his movements on the night of the killing. What does he do? First, something unexpected. He makes a tentative attempt to break into Harrisons. He knows we've gone over the house with several combs, yet still his first move is trying to break in there. Now why would that be?'

He looked at Gissing. Gissing frowned and shifted his feet. 'I don't know . . . perhaps something he left there. Something we aren't on to yet.'

'You mean, that might incriminate him?'

Gissing nodded cautiously. 'Him or the murderer. That's how it looks. Or could be just he was on the make . . . he wasn't particular what he pinched.'

Gently shrugged. 'We'll leave that too! But it led to an encounter between me and Colkett. As a result, he probably got the idea that we were ready to pounce on him. The cosh he didn't think we'd find, but he couldn't bear to chuck away the coin, so he caught the next bus into Norchester and turned the coin into cash.

'Up till then, I don't think Colkett had any settled notion of skipping. It takes a lot to shift a fellow like him, who has lived all his life in a small town. He was in trouble, but he had a ready tongue, and the coin was all that could've linked him with Peachment. Now he was clear of it: he could come back and flannel along as best he might. But then he turned the corner of Playford Road, and saw Metcalfe waiting there to grab him. Why? Only one reason – we'd found out about him selling the coin! Now he is scared. The coin is damning. He can't spruce his way round that. Standing in the snow on the corner, Colkett realizes it must be flight.'

Gently paused.

'Now consider a moment the situation Colkett is faced with. He's just walked two miles through a blizzard, and he knows the roads outside are impassable. The trains may or may not be running, but it's pretty certain we'll be watching them. And in his pocket he's got forty-odd quid – not very much for a man on the run! He's stuck – and he needs two things: shelter for the night, and more cash. The first, if he's lucky, he can get at the warehouse. But the second . . . what about that?'

Brewer whistled softly. 'Reckon you've got it, sir.'

Gently nodded. 'It's a fair bet.'

'But,' Gissing said, 'what was he after? There's nothing in the house – I'm ready to swear to it.'

184

Gently gestured impatiently. 'That didn't matter! The point is that Colkett *believed* there was something. The kids had sold him the notion that Peachment had a hoard, and his finding the coin there had made it gospel. In the morning, he'd gone there to have a scout round, perhaps only to see if he could spot the hiding-place. But by the evening he was in deadly earnest – somehow, he had to get his hands on those coins.

'Which of course tells us something interesting. Colkett knew the murderer didn't get the coins. If they'd ever existed, they were still in the house . . . Colkett, the murderer, both knew it.'

'Jesus – and Colkett walked into him!' Brewer exclaimed.

'The other way round,' Gently said. 'Colkett broke in, we know that, so the murderer must have walked into Colkett.' He hesitated. 'It calls for a coincidence,' he said.

'But hell – it happened, sir!' Brewer said eagerly.

Gently shrugged. 'Colkett chased those kids . . . he may have shown himself in Thingoe Road.'

He was silent for a little, sitting drooped, staring at the oddments on the desk.

'The murderer isn't very tall,' he said. 'It could be a woman, but I think it's a man. Not very tall, not very powerful, does his work with furious hitting. Peachment caught him and got in his way. The murderer kept hitting Peachment, driving him backwards. Then Peachment fell, which may have been accidental, but with Colkett it was deliberate: Colkett had come for the gold.'

Gissing gave a little groan. 'And you think . . . Thingoe Road?'

'A short man,' Gently said. 'Perhaps one who nobody would think to fear.'

'We'll find him,' Brewer said. 'We'll find him, sir.'

Gently nodded, got to his feet. 'Thingoe Road . . . house by house. Whoever was out in the snow that night.'

Reporters were waiting in reception and Gently gave them a brief, tight statement. They had their teeth in this one now and showed it by insistent and ingenious questioning. Gently had fobbed them off before – he wouldn't get away with it twice! Unless he wanted a bad press he'd better play ball, come across with the hard stuff . . .

He got shot of them at last and escaped into the twilit streets. A slow thaw had begun: it was like a cattleyard underfoot. Filthy cars went sloshing by, swidging snow-mud onto the pavements, and a few wretched pedestrains slunk along close to the walls. Gently slithered his way across the market place and down into the funnel of Water Street. It suited his mood, this . . . the darkening wilderness of foul ways. It was the right setting for the crime at Harrisons, inhuman, corrosive, anti-life: rotting snow, rotting life. And the dark coming down again.

He came to Bressingham's little courtyard and drew off the street into it. Hard edges of cartwheels and the head of a statue broke through the snow that choked most of the enclosure. Bressingham had shovelled a broad path from the shop door to the pavement, and

186

cleared the area before the window. But no customer was peering at his rings.

Gently pushed open the chiming door. Bressingham was sitting at the counter, an evening paper spread before him. He was leaning on his elbows, shoulders round, pince-nez low on his button nose. He looked up quickly.

'Hullo, Superintendent . . . oh, my gosh! This terrible business.'

Gently nodded and closed the door. He came up slowly to the counter.

'I'm just reading here . . . of course, I'd heard about it. They took my fingerprints, you know that? . . . but, oh, goodness. I'd got the idea that Colkett was the man you fancied.'

'I didn't say so,' Gently said.

'No – you wouldn't, would you?' Bressingham said. 'But reading between the lines – and I'm a professional! – that was the impression you gave me. And now . . . ugh – the poor devil. I wish I hadn't told you about him. He was a worthless sort of creature, perhaps, but . . . gosh, he didn't deserve this.'

'Nor did Peachment,' Gently said.

'Well, no – nor Peachment neither. But somehow, Peachment . . . he was older, I suppose. It seemed to make it a little less ghastly.'

Bressingham leaned back, staring up at Gently, grey eyes questioning behind their lenses. His plump hands lay together on the counter, the sensitive fingers stirring slightly.

'You here on business?'

Gently shrugged. 'I have to put my man in a cell.'

Bressingham shivered. 'That sounds so . . . inexorable. I don't think I could ever do your job. How can I help?'

Gently looked away from him. 'We want information about Thursday evening. We're asking everyone, trying to build a picture. Between the hours of seven and nine.'

'Seven and nine.' Bressingham paused. 'Curious,' he said. 'They were both killed around then. But I'm no good, I didn't go out. Ursy and I were in all evening.'

'You didn't go for a drink?'

'Have a heart! It was snowing fit to break the bank. As a matter of fact I was delving in Blomefield, trying to find that Latin for you.'

'Yes . . . I'd forgotten.'

Bressingham chuckled. 'Ursy won't have forgotten,' he said. 'I was really sore with myself that night. She had to drive me off to bed.'

'You were on it all the evening?'

'More or less. After Phil was packed off.'

'When does he go to bed?'

'Oh, sevenish. But the young devil sits up there reading.' Bressingham's eyes twinkled. 'He's a chip of the old 'un,' he said. 'Ursy, I mean – not me. He'll be a sharp one when he grows up.'

'Does he fuss about bedtime?'

'He's pretty good. Ursy puts him through his drill.'

'His bath and that?'

Bressingham nodded, his eyes smiling to themselves. Gently said nothing. He leaned on the counter, his eyes wandering over its furniture: a coin-cabinet, a mirror, a day-book, a little stack of printed pamphlets. He paused at the latter. The pamphlets were headed: WANTED – GOLD! – and listed items that Bressingham wished to purchase. Gently picked one up. He could sense the dealer watching him closely.

'Just a bit of nonsense to stick in parcels. It ties in with my press adverts.'

'Neat,' Gently said. 'Printed locally?'

'Better still. I do them myself.'

'You!'

'Don't sound so shocked! I have an old flatbed I bought at an auction. Are you interested in printing?'

Gently's stare was hard. 'Sometimes,' he said. 'May I take one of these?'

Bressingham waved the request aside. Gently put the pamphlet in his wallet. Bressingham glanced fondly for a moment at the stack on the counter, then looked up at Gently, eyes serious.

'But this isn't helping you very much ... do you think I might ask a naughty question?'

'I may not answer it.'

'A nod, you old fox! Do you know who it is?'

Their eyes held. Slowly, Gently nodded.

'Aha,' Bressingham said. 'And you're nearly home.'

'Nearly,' Gently said. He turned away. 'One more step.'

Bressingham was silent.

From outside came the muted slushing of the cars in Water Street. Down the shop a clock tocked hollowly, measuring rotund, unhurried seconds.

'Tonight,' Gently said, 'I think I'll go ghost-watching. It's time I met the spectre of Harrisons.'

'Oh, glory!' Bressingham exclaimed. 'Would you like me to come along?'

Gently shook his head. 'Just me. It mightn't walk if there were a crowd. About eight seems to be the witching hour. I'll be on the lookout soon after seven.'

'But . . . will it be safe?' Bressingham queried.

Gently shrugged. 'I've got strong nerves! And I'll spend the waiting-time probing that storeroom . . . just in case the gold is still there.'

'Oh Lord, it's mad!' Bressingham wailed. 'At least you'll have men on call somewhere?'

Gently shook his head again. 'Fair play,' he said. 'Even for ghosts.'

He went back to the George for a bite to eat – somehow lunch had got missed out – and had them send it to his room, where he was safe from the reporters. He had small appetite. He sat eating by his window, which looked down on the morass of Water Street. A droning monster was crawling in the street, creaming the snow-slush towards the pavements. All it needed now was a frost . . . He lit his pipe, still watching. No appetite! Just a sick emptiness deep down in his guts . . .

He rang the desk. There was no message – but what message was he expecting? Even when he'd sent the others to Thingoe Road he'd known he was getting them out of the way. Suddenly, the affair had become personal, a matter between himself and the murderer

. . . as perhaps it had been all along, though he'd only just realized it. Well, Thingoe Road had to be combed: that was justifiable routine!

And yet, wasn't he hoping for some message, waiting idly as the minutes sped by . . . hoping still that the dogged Gissing would turn up a fresh, decisive lead? He knew he was. Like a condemned man, he was holding on for a reprieve, giving the chances these few last moments to turn up the miracle that sometimes happened . . .

But the phone stayed silent. His watch showed seven. He rose, and knocked out his pipe. Going down the stairs, he noticed reporters standing gossiping in the hall lounge. He slipped into the dining-room, which was empty, and gained the courtyard through the kitchen. Nobody saw him climb in the Sceptre and glide softly on his way.

CHAPTER FOURTEEN

T HE PANDA CAR had been withdrawn and Harrisons stood without a guardian. Only a little light from the lamp in the passage spread thinly into the yard. Gently drove round the yard in a tight circle, with crisping snow crumbling under his wheels, parked, cut his lights, sat for a short while looking and listening. Nothing stirring, here or in Frenze Street, nor in the pale waste of the sale-ground. The snows, the night had already closed in, shutting life away from the spot. He got out, deliberately slamming his door. The bang might have acted as a cue. At the end of the passage, plain in the lamplight, appeared Dinno, Moosh, and two of the kids. Gently waited. They stared interestedly, then advanced a few yards up the passage. Gently went down towards them. He met them under the lamp.

'Hullo, mister . . . found him yet?'

Gently shook his head. 'Who, Dinno?'

'Him what done it – murdered old Cokey. Don't reckon he just fell down them stairs.'

He looked steadily at Gently, man to man, his face wan in the lamplight. Moosh, less bold, was punting snow, and the other two gazed with their witless gaze.

'Do you know who it is, Dinno?' Gently said.

'Me – how should I know?' Dinno said. 'Reckon it was Cokey who murdered old Peachey. Reckon it was him what had the gold.'

'No,' Gently said. 'He didn't have the gold.'

'That's what we reckon,' Dinno asserted obstinately.

'Nobody had the gold, did they?' Gently said.

Dinno stared at him with resentful eyes.

'Nobody had the gold,' Gently said. 'But you kidded someone, and they tried to get it. And I think you know who that someone is. And I think you could tell me if you wanted to.'

Dinno shook his head. 'Don't know, mister.'

'Yes,' Gently said. 'Yes, you know.'

'Cut my throat, mister . . . ask anyone.'

'Tha's right,' Moosh said. 'We don't know, mister.'

Gently shrugged. 'It doesn't matter now . . . perhaps we know who he is anyway. And the gold, we'll soon find out about that. It's just a pity you won't come clean.'

Dinno's eyes wavered, then sank. 'We don't know nothing, mister,' he mumbled.

Gently nodded. 'All right. Run along. It's time you fellows were home by the fire.'

They turned and trooped away silently, heads hanging, feet slouching. At the end of the passage Dinno looked back. Then they vanished into Thingoe Road.

The lock-assembly had been renewed on the back door of Harrisons, and after letting himself in, Gently slipped the padlock in his pocket. He'd brought a hand-lamp from the Sceptre. It lit up the seedy rooms with a flitting garishness. The house was colder than it had ever been and still with a listening house-stillness. He went through the kitchen to the back corridor. There was no longer snow-water on the bare boards. A lighter patch, opposite the foot of the stairs, marked the spot where Colkett's blood had been expunged. Going up the stairs, he tested each one to discover if it had a warning creak, but though they were old they were damp and tight, and it was only a board on the landing that responded. Not much of a warning there! The door with its letters had been left closed. Stooping, Gently put his hand through the aperture and felt for the bolt – yes; it checked.

He went in. Was there any real point in examining that tiresome room again? At the bottom of him, he knew he had ceased to believe in the Harrison hoard and its hiding-place. A hiding-place was fundamentally a nuisance, a place to secure things you didn't much handle; for things you did handle, perhaps daily, you used a strong-room – and this was a strong-room. No: the collection had sat on the shelves in the days of its eccentric owner, and had vanished away at his death, leaving only the tale behind.

He set the hand-lamp on the deal table, where its light would be visible from the yard, then lit his pipe and tried to settle to the business of waiting and listening. But still his eyes kept wandering round the room, probing, sifting its barren features. Just because it was so bare and simple . . . could there be a trick to it . . . somewhere?

In effect it had only two features, the door and the shelves in the toe of the L. They were both on the one side, with about a yard of blank wall between them. The shelves were as plain as shelves could be, supported by bearers attached to the wainscot. The door, on the other hand, was redundantly elaborate, a massive framework of many panels. If there was a trick where would it be? Certainly, it couldn't be in the door. That left the shelves as the single possibility, the shelves which Bressingham had tested so thoroughly.

Frowning, Gently caught up the lamp and played its beam along the shelves. There was a spot on the wainscot, he remembered, where Bressingham's raps had produced a resonance. He began tapping softly with his knuckles. The spot was between the two centre shelves. It was barely detectable, but quite extensive, sounding over most of the area bounded by the shelves. Defective brickwork? Dry rot? The wainscot looked solid and healthy. Gently tested the shelves as Bressingham had done, with the same result: they were quite firm. He proceeded to the remaining shelves and wainscot, but could find nothing else suggestive. He shrugged. If there was a trick, you would need a hammer and chisel to work it.

He relit his pipe, and listened some moments to the close, still, silence. It was seven-thirty. If the ghost were walking, it ought to be putting its chains on now.

But he heard no sound. The house, the street might have been in the depths of the country. He flashed the lamp down the stairs. Nothing. He was alone in the silence, the frosty night.

Softly, he closed the heavy door and let the light fall on its many panels. Was it just credible that the trick was here, in this Portal of Olympus? No doubt old Harrison had designed that door, and had it hung there on its smith-made hinges – where, for around three hundred years, it had faithfully and cleanly opened and closed. The frame was thick . . . Gently fingered the panels. Possible to have inserted compartments in those? To have made the door itself a safe, of which the brass plate had formed a key? There'd been twenty-six letters on the brass plate, but the panels numbered only eighteen . . . and their joints were sealed with some ancient varnish, had not been disturbed in this century. He fondled the bolt, sliding it gently into its socket in the jamb. At the end of its travel it resisted slightly, then went home with a faint click. The result of wear? He tried it again. This time he felt no resistance, but on releasing the knob he heard the click again, and the knob jerked back about half an inch. For a second he stared at it, then he pulled open the door and shone his lamp into the socket. At the end of the socket he could see protruding a thick tongue of metal. He took out a nail-file and pushed the tongue with it: the tongue clicked back and stayed put. He pushed again: the tongue depressed slightly, clicked, and sprang out. A trick indeed! But what sort of trick? What was the mechanism supposed to operate? He pushed in the

196

tongue very, very slowly, scrutinizing the door-frame as the click occurred. But nothing happened, nothing moved: he just heard that tantalizing sound.

One more of Harrisons' inexplicable mysteries?

He drew back from the door with a grunt of irritation. Yet it had to work something, that obscure little gimmick . . . if not around the door, then some place . . . somewhere . . .

And in a sudden surge, he knew he had it. The door, the shelves – they formed one unit! Only three feet distance intervened between the socket in the jamb and the central shelves . . .

Leaving the tongue pushed in, he moved to the shelves, grasped one in each hand and gave a jerk. Shelves, wainscot, drew out in a rigid box, sliding freely on the bearers of the lower shelf.

And there it stood in the grimy cavity: a small, nail-studded, leather-covered coffer, with silver initials on the rounded lid . . . and fresh chew-marks above the lock.

Gently fetched the chair and stood the lamp on it. Full or empty – that was the question! Had Peachment managed to keep his secret, or had blows from the cosh jerked it out of his throat?

He tipped the lid back: the coffer was full.

Inside, it was nested with leather-lined trays. In the top tray lay a confusion of dulled gold pieces, mingling with crumpled squares of the famous blue paper. Gently lifted the tray out. Its weight astonished him. In the next tray the pieces were still mostly wrapped. On

197

each wrapping, he noticed, a description was written with a spidery pen, in an ink gone brown. And so with the next tray, and the next: old Peachment had sampled one here and there. But the weight told you – it was gold, and more gold: ten brutal trays of it, stacked one on the other. And there it had lain, in the gloomy coffer, while Harrison's heirs had come and gone, through reigns and centuries, deaths and entrances, till the deaf old man had jemmied-in daylight . . .

And he? He'd left it lying, perhaps with a chuckle at his own astuteness, with a little fond wonderment that such things were, and a whimsical hint to his straight-faced nephew. Sell it? Be rich? What would it buy him? Trouble, anxiety and loss of quiet . . . no! The old man wasn't such a fool. And perhaps he'd have let the secret die with him.

Sombrely, Gently replaced the trays. Alas, old Peachment hadn't kept the secret. He'd shown a tiny corner of that gold, curious to know what the stuff was worth. And then, at a curtainless window, he'd pored over the coins, examining the kings and queens and emperors – and the tale was out. Twenty-four hours later his corpse was stretched at the foot of the stairs.

For gold . . .

This soft rotten metal, in which men had rested their ugliest madness.

Kill for this? What was it?

It didn't even make a serviceable coin!

He slammed the lid down, and turned his attention to the sliding shelves again. They were beautifully crafted, and so arranged that their thickness concealed the breaks in the wainscot. The upper bearers were integral and embodied a small brass socket. This mated with a rod, also brass, which emerged from a collar in the wall. You entered the room, bolted the door, and the shelves were free to be withdrawn; you left the room, bolted the door, and the shelves were automatically locked. Unless you knew to bolt the door when you entered, passing the Portal of Olympus would get you nowhere . . . .

He lifted back the shelves and slid them home. Now the secret rested with him! Locked or unlocked, the shelves defied even the most expert examination.

At that moment the board on the landing creaked. He swung quickly to face the door. And his blood stood still.

He saw Dinno crouching there, and behind Dinno, Moosh and the rest of the gang.

They had the coshes, the green coshes, and they huddled watching him with dead eyes. Dinno was swinging his cosh rhythmically, his gaze somehow going past Gently. They had the togetherness of a strange animal, stupid, poised for a kill. They weren't children any longer: they were violence, waiting to erupt.

He felt a chill colder than the frost, a rush of paralysing horror . . .

Dinno's hand flicked. The cosh flew. The bolt struck Gently in the forehead. Blood rippled down between his eyes and he staggered, his knees going weak. Then they were on him, hitting him, battering him, welting the strength out of his body, with just the trampling and grunting and thudding as the coshes rose and fell.

'Get the old bugger to the door!'

Panting savagely, they began to drive him. Like Colkett . . . with, like Colkett, blood pouring down over his nose . . .

'Come on . . . he'll go the same way!'

And the horror showing in his face . . . like Colkett, like Peachment . . . and no attempt to defend himself.

With a great effort he seized on the chair and jabbed its legs into the attackers. They fell back squealing, oddly weightless, while the lamp went scuttling into a corner.

'Get him . . . get the old sod . . . !'

He jabbed again, producing howls. He backed out of the L and towards the doorway, taking vicious blows as he went.

'Now . . . now we've got him!'

But they hadn't. He swung the chair in two desperate sweeps. Then, throwing it at them, he staggered on to the landing, dragged the door shut, and turned the key.

'The old bugger . . . the old bugger . . . !'

A hand shot through the aperture, feeling for the key. Just in time, Gently whipped the key out and tremblingly slipped it into his pocket. Fists, feet battered on the door. Voices shouted and wailed, childishly grotesque.

'You let us out . . . let us out . . . !'

He stumbled, went down the stairs in a kind of sobbing hysteria.

In the Sceptre, he pulled himself together and got the R/T working. He made his voice firm, forced it steady to give a few hoarse instructions. Then he sat back, eyes closed, trying to shrink from the aches of his body. Oh, God . . . but there might be still another quirk to this business . . .

He started the engine and drove shakily away, to park again when he reached Bressingham's. The shop was dark, but he could see light outlining the curtain at the back. He rang and kept ringing. After a while the curtain stirred. Bressingham, jacketless and in slippers, switched on the lights and crossed to the door. He saw Gently.

'Oh . . . holy Jesus!'

He came out quickly and grabbed Gently's arm. He lugged him hastily into the shop, kicking the door shut behind them.

'Christ . . . what's happened?'

Gently stared at him, feeling Bressingham's horrified eyes on the blood.

'Your son – *where is he*?'

'Phil . . . ? In bed. But—'

Gently just nodded, leaning hard on the counter.

Ursula Bressingham came round the curtain. Her black eyes gazed hotly at Gently. She stared silently, very still. Then she shrugged.

'You'd better come in. I'll fix you up.'

There were ten of them who slunk wailing and blubbering out of the old eccentric's strong-room, and they passed down the stairs into an anonymity which the Press reluctantly respected. But the Press quickly found a tag for them. They were dubbed 'the Cross Innocents' – which soon became, simply, the 'Innocents'; Cross having little appeal to the mass-memory.

And the coins, they were sold by Sotheby's, and realized one-and-three-quarter million pounds. Gently, who found them, received nothing, neither did Bressingham, who'd pointed the way; but the latter, in a moment of rashness, bought the Edward IV angel under the hammer.

Rigby House,
Norwich.
18.11.68/3.3.69